ULTIMATE ENDING

BOOK 1

TREASURES
OF THE
FORGOTTEN CITY

Check out the full

ULTIMATE ENDING BOOKS

Series:

TREASURES OF THE FORGOTTEN CITY

THE HOUSE ON HOLLOW HILL

THE SHIP AT THE EDGE OF TIME

ENIGMA AT THE GREENSBORO ZOO

THE SECRET OF THE AURORA HOTEL

THE STRANGE PHYSICS OF THE HEIDELBERG LABORATORY

THE TOWER OF NEVER THERE

Cover design by Xia Taptara www.xiataptara.com

Internal artwork by Jaime Buckley www.jaimebuckley.com

Enjoyed this book? Please take the time to leave a review on Amazon.

For my wife, Aurelia. Still the best treasure I've ever found.

Welcome to **Ultimate Ending,**
where YOU choose the story!

That's right – everything that happens in this book is a result of
decisions YOU make. So choose wisely!

But also be careful. Throughout this book you'll find tricks and traps,
trials and tribulations! Most you can avoid with common sense and a
logical approach to problem solving. Others will require a little bit of luck.
Having a coin handy, or a pair of dice, will make your adventure even more
fun. So grab em' if you got em'!

Along the way you'll also find tips, clues, and even items that can help
you in your quest. You'll meet people. Pick stuff up. Taking note of these
things is often important, so while you're gathering your courage, you
might also want to grab yourself a pencil and a sheet of paper.

Keep in mind, there are *many* ways to end the story. Some conclusions
are good... some not so good.
Some of them are even great!
But remember:

There is only *ONE*

ULTIMATE
ENDING!

Welcome to the Arabian Desert!

You are DONOVAN YOUNG, entrepreneur, explorer, and most recently, would-be treasure hunter. For the past six weeks you've been working hard to fulfill your grand-uncle's unrealized dream; finding *ATRAHARSIS* – the legendary city beneath the sands.

You were always adventurous, and never missed an opportunity to listen to your grand-uncle's tales of traveling the world. As his favorite nephew he left you a journal; the diary of Robert Murdoch, a man who once claimed to have found Atraharsis and then lost it again. The journal contains clues, most in the form of riddles themselves. Included with the journal is a thick piece of triangular sandstone, covered in glyphs, which your grand-uncle always claimed was the key to entering the city.

Unfortunately, finding the city is proving a lot harder than you originally thought. Since his passing, your grand-uncle's estate has fallen into financial ruin. You've used the last of his resources to fund your expedition, but with the money now gone and the supplies run out, your crew has finally abandoned you. Only by securing one or more of Atraharsis's three priceless star jewels, once gifted to the city's greatest monarchs, can you hope to save your grand-uncle's legacy.

This is your third night alone in the desert and a raging sandstorm ravages your small camp. All you can do is ride it out, huddling up in your tent as the wind rips mercilessly at the thick canvas seams. One peg comes loose. Then two. The entire canopy fills with a blast of air and you have a brief, terrifying vision of the whole tent being uprooted and flung into the desert sky.

8

You scramble to your feet! But before you can do anything the flap of your tent swings open and a man enters.

He's small. Scrawny. Covered from head to toe in dust and sand. You don't recognize him as one of your former crew, but it makes little difference. The man spits a mouthful of dirt before quickly getting to work securing the loose tent posts. You join him, and together you barely manage to keep your small canvas shelter from being torn from the ground.

"I am Waif," he coughs finally. Outside the storm still howls, furious at being defeated. "Actually my name is Renn, but they *call* me Waif. The others, I mean."

You look the man up and down as he dusts himself off. He must be one of Sullivan's crew. The opposing dig team caused you a lot of worry when they first showed up over a week ago. Now, you suppose, it doesn't really matter.

"I'm Donovan. Donovan Young. Mind if I ask how you got here?"

"I left the other expedition," Waif explains. "The other men and I had... differences." He sighs and lowers his head in admission. "In truth I was cast out. Mr. Sullivan would not listen to me. He digs too far to the north, and he operates under dangerously foolish conditions."

"Well I'm sure glad you showed up," you say. Waif returns your smile weakly. The storm passes and the hours tick by. By morning you know all about the other dig team, including how many of your men Sullivan managed to pick up. Sadly you think back to your grand-uncle. To his old manor house, empty now except for a whole lifetime's worth of his personal treasures.

"The best I can do is offer you breakfast," you tell Waif as you step from the tent. "I was actually about to pack up and–"

An object catches your eye, silhouetted against the golden sliver of rising sun. Something is poking up from the sands...

"Waif," you cry out in excitement. "Come on!"

Together you bound over to the object, a large four-sided obelisk jutting straight up from the sands. It's covered on all sides with strange glyphs and markings. Some of them you recognize from your grand-uncle's journal.

"What is it?" asks Waif.

"I don't know, but it wasn't here yesterday." All around the obelisk is a base of solid bedrock. The sand is pushed back in every direction.

"The storm," Waif offers. "Maybe the winds uncovered it?"

You run your hand over the ancient column, which towers a good six feet above your head. Right around eye level you notice a very familiar, triangular-shaped hole.

"The key!" you gasp. Adrenaline surges through you as you pull the thick piece of stone from your rucksack. "This must be the lock! The key fits right–"

"Hold on," Waif warns. "Look – there are holes like this on all four sides. How do you know which side it belongs in?"

He's right. Each hole is the exact same shape as the piece of stone your grand-uncle gave you. You glance down at the journal, searching for answers. There you find a sketch... and a riddle:

North, South, East, West
One Brings Life, The Others Death
Sun and Moon and Stars Bereft
The One Right Way is Not the Left

You look back at the obelisk. "Each of its sides are aligned to the four points of the compass," you say.

10

Below the riddle is a crude drawing. You wonder if it was sketched by Robert Murdoch himself.

"What does *'bereft'* mean?" Waif asks.

"It means 'without'," you say absently. And with your own answer, realization suddenly dawns over you. "Waif, I get it! We need to choose the side without the sun or moon or stars!"

Together you circle the obelisk. Just above each of the four keyholes is a mark. On the east face is the sun glyph. Opposite that, on the west, is a moon. A mark symbolizing the stars appears on the south side, and on the north...

"Here," you tell Waif. "The crown. It's gotta be the crown."

You reach up and plug the stone key into the obelisk. Nothing happens.

"Perhaps you have to turn it," Waif suggests.

Well, it looks like you have two choices.

If you turn the obelisk key clockwise, *HEAD OVER TO PAGE 47*

If you turn the key counter-clockwise instead, *FLIP ON DOWN TO PAGE 153*

You don't know much about jackals, but you do know something about dogs. And turning your back on a pack of charging hounds is probably the worst thing you can do at this point.

"HA!" you scream as loud as you can. "HAAA! HAAAAA!"

You pull your camping hatchet from your rucksack, never taking your eyes from the lead dog. By standing up straight, and flaring your shoulders, you try to make yourself look as menacing as possible.

"HAAA!" Waif repeats a little more awkwardly. His height and stature are unfortunate in this situation, but your partner has the advantage of his torch. The flames leave a trail of greasy black smoke as he waves it before him in a wide arc.

The combined display gives the jackals pause. They halt their advance and begin growling suspiciously, side-stepping in a circle as they try to gain position. But they're still coming...

All of a sudden something flies through the air. There's a loud thump, and the dogs leap off to one side. The snarling is replaced by snapping and biting as the three of them fight tooth and nail in the desert sand.

You back up slowly. Incredibly, the jackals don't even notice you anymore.

"What in the world was that?"

"A haunch of goat," Waif replies. He wipes a greasy hand on his pack as he closes it. "*Spiced* goat."

Ugh. You're caught between being grateful and feeling sorry for the poor animals. But hey, at least you're still in one piece.

Nice job sticking up for yourself! Now *TURN TO PAGE 118*

12

Waif reaches out and grabs your arm... but you're too heavy. He doesn't have the strength to hold you, and together the two of you go rolling down the side of the Ziggurat!

The whole world becomes a blur of light and noise. You tumble for what seems like forever, giving your body up to gravity, trying to stay loose enough that you don't break anything. A bed of jagged rock guides you painfully down the stone pyramid, but it also slows your fall. The friction eventually brings you to a sharp, grinding halt.

The next thing you know Waif is standing over you. You stand up, brush yourself off, and take stock of the situation. You're alive, and you appear to be intact. Ditto for Waif. For now at least, it seems you're both okay.

"I suppose we'll be taking your way," says Waif. He points to the dark opening in the Ziggurat. It's only a few steps above where your fall ended.

You nod at him and then cough. Something shifts uncomfortably behind your ribs.

"Let's do it," you say. "Before the pain kicks in."

You can head into the heart of the Ziggurat by *GOING TO PAGE 114*

Hurrying through the city, you're still out of breath when a crude structure juts skyward in the road ahead. Tall and lean, it appears to be made of several large stones fitted carefully together. It also seems oddly familiar.

"This is the monolith," you say, pulling out your grand-uncle's journal. "See? Here it is on the map."

Surrounding the strange totem are three smaller towers of stacked stone. Two of them seem to have fallen over a long time ago. A third one still stands, but only partially.

"The journal talks about this place," you tell Waif, "but in the form of a riddle." You open to the page read the following passage aloud:

Six Spokes Around a Buried Wheel
Three Glyphs of Certain Doom
Tread Wisely Down the Path of Kings
Step Wrong and Seal Your Tomb

"It makes no sense," says Waif. "There are three spokes here, and no wheel. And nothing is buried."

The two of you pace slowly around the monolith in contemplation. In doing so you notice that each fallen tower bears a mark – or glyph – carved beneath it. One of the marks is a horse. The second one is a hawk.

"Are these the 'glyphs of certain doom'?" Waif asks nervously.

"I don't know," you reply, "but I'm writing them all down." You notice your partner doesn't appear very happy at the news.

"Should we knock this one down as well?" Waif finally asks, pointing out the third tower. "More than likely there will be another glyph beneath it."

Odds are he's probably right. The column of stacked stone already leans precariously to one side. But it also looks dangerously unstable.

Do you help Waif topple the third tower? If so *FLIP ON DOWN TO PAGE 128*
Or maybe you'd rather leave well enough alone. If that's the case, *TURN TO PAGE 41*

14

The dust envelops you, despite your best attempts at avoiding it. It shimmers. It glimmers. It's horridly beautiful... at least up until you blink, and your eyes suddenly feel like they're being sliced by a thousand tiny razors.

"Waif!" you scream, but it's already too late. Your friend is face down on the floor, unmoving. Malevolent green light continues streaming into the chamber, reminding you of your failure. It's the last thing you see before your eyesight is taken away, signifying that this is indeed

THE END

Slowly, without taking your eyes from the cheetah's, you draw forth your canteen and uncap it. Then, as vigorously as possible, you shake a bunch of water in the direction of its face.

Nothing happens.

The cat screams in anger. Waif is staring at you like you just grew three extra heads. Silently you curse yourself as you drop the canteen to the floor of the cave.

Did you really just do that? Let's pretend you didn't. Choose again:

Try fighting the cheetah off with a torch by *TURNING TO PAGE 42*

Or you can run blindly into the next cave by *HEADING OVER TO PAGE 95*

16

"Stay here," you tell Waif. "And back me up if anything goes wrong."

You back away slowly and circle around the outside perimeter of the fire pit. No one's ever accused you of being light on your feet, but the sand muffles your footsteps to where you feel like you're being sufficiently stealthy. By the time you get to the opposite side of the circle, the dark figure hasn't moved. He stands there perfectly still, leaning casually against the pillar.

Without thinking you rush him. You're not sure why, but for some reason it seems important to have the element of surprise. The figure does absolutely nothing as you approach. Either that, or he doesn't even see you...

At the last possible second you realize your mistake. You change direction, and rather than slam full force into the pillar itself you go sprawling headlong into the fire pit. Dust and dirt fly everywhere. You also enjoy the distinctly new sensation of getting sand up your nose.

You're brushing off the last of the charcoal as Waif runs up to you. He's laughing.

"He's over there," he points. Off to your right, the statue of a scholarly man stands tall on a worn pedestal. "If you hurry you can still catch him!"

You return Waif's humor with a twisted smirk. The figure on the pillar was nothing more than a shadow!

"At least you searched the fire pit," Waif quips. "Come. We haven't checked these roads yet."

Two very broad avenues lead away from the fire pit.

If you take the west road, *TURN TO PAGE 124*

If you head east instead, *GO TO PAGE 103*

You look at Waif and laugh. "You're being silly, man. We could use some luck."

With that you flip the quarter high into the air. It catches the sun for one gleaming instant, then drops into the four-thousand year old well. The two of you look at each other, half expecting something to happen. Nothing does.

"I didn't hear it hit bottom," Waif says.

"Probably landed in the sand."

The two of you lean over the well shaft one last time in an effort to see something. As you do, Waif's torch illuminates three distinct symbols carved side-by-side into the stone: an owl eating a snake eating a rodent.

"What's that about?" you ask.

Waif shrugs. "I don't know. Circle of life?" He seems a lot more relieved now that the coin-toss is over. "Say, what did you wish for anyway?"

You laugh again, this time patting him on the back so hard he almost falls over. "Can't tell you or it won't come true."

Hey, a rule is a rule. Now *TURN TO PAGE 33*

18

The avenue you're walking widens into a broad concourse. Soon a structure looms in the distance, tall and impressive and leaping up toward the sky. The shape is unmistakable. When you were young, your grand-uncle must've pointed it out to you a hundred different times on Murdoch's map.

"The Ziggurat!"

The massive, multi-tiered pyramid is a darker stone than the rest of the city. You wonder where the giant stone blocks were cut from, how they got here, who built the thing and why. Too many questions. Too long ago.

"Your map has one of the star jewels next to the Ziggurat," Waif says. "Perhaps it's inside?"

"That's what I'm counting on," you tell him. If Waif were to look down at your hands right now, he'd find your fingers crossed. "Alright, let's get climbing."

There are a series of stone steps leading up all four sides of the pyramid. The south side seems to be the least dangerous. Your climb is slow, the slope uncomfortably steep. The steps are mostly covered in sand, which makes it difficult to get any sort of decent footing.

"C'mon," Waif calls back from ahead of you. "We're almost there."

A rock-slide of small boulders rumbles past you as Waif nears the top. It takes some maneuvering, but you manage to get out of the way in time. The last quarter of the climb however, appears exceptionally treacherous. Many of the stones look cracked and loose. Then, something catches your eye.

"Hang on, I think I found something."

There's an opening in the Ziggurat's face. You stare into it and see nothing but blackness.

"There's a room here," you call up to Waif. Smaller and lighter (not to mention a better climber), he's just about at the top. "Maybe we can use it to gain access to the upper chambers?"

If you decide to call Waif down and try to find another way up from inside the Ziggurat, *FLIP TO PAGE 114*

Then again, you're almost there. If you want to take a chance with those last few steps, *GO TO PAGE 73*

20

There's something you like about the horse glyph... something innocuous and non-threatening. For some odd reason, it just seems like it would be the right choice.

"Let's try this one," you tell Waif.

Together you pass beneath the horse symbol, into the shadows. The hall continues onward for a long while, curving left as you go. You pass several side-corridors, but all of them are caved in. Perhaps they once went somewhere, but right now they're packed with nothing but rubble and cobwebs.

Side by side you continue walking, sticking to the main tunnel. Eventually, the corridor ends. The room ahead is total darkness. You step forward and enter it, heart pounding...

This is it! This must be–

"We're back in the same room!" Waif says. The torchlight reveals the hexagonal chamber exactly the same as you left it. Waif looks absolutely stunned.

You take the torch from him and hold it over your head. Directly above, the serpent glyph stares down at you. It looks poised and ready to strike.

"We walked in a circle," you say. "The horse and the snake must be the same corridor. They're connected."

Waif scratches his head. "Well at least our odds just got better. We eliminated two possibilities."

He's right! There are only four exits left to choose from.

If you pick the exit marked with the DOG, *TURN TO PAGE 146*
If you pick the exit marked with the CROWN, *TURN TO PAGE 99*
If you pick the exit marked with the CAT, *TURN TO PAGE 156*
If you pick the exit marked with the HAWK, *TURN TO PAGE 160*

Here the street widens into a long, broad concourse. Large granite statues tower over both sides of the avenue, each carved in exquisite, painstaking detail. They appear to depict the Sultans, Khans, and many rulers of Atraharsis. None bear weapons. Most bear scrolls, staffs, and even tools in some cases. All of them look distinguished, amiable, and wise.

You've passed at least two dozen such statues, including more than a few women, when you finally turn to Waif. "How many leaders of Atraharsis were there?"

"These are not the leaders," he corrects you. "These were the scholars, the teachers, the passers of knowledge. There was a time, long ago, when they were revered even above kings and queens."

At the end of the avenue, a lone statue presides over the center. A series of glyphs are carved deeply into the base. Waif impresses you by translating them roughly:

Gold, jewels, armies, land – false tenements of true power
Cities fall. Kings perish. Dynasties crumble. Linage ends
These things are constructs of man. Always fleeting
Only knowledge is forever

You let out a long breath. "That's deep."

"Deep?"

"Yeah. These people were gravely serious about their culture. Whatever happened to them?"

Waif shrugs. "Perhaps they were conquered. Or the aquifer running beneath the city finally dried up. There are many such theories." He pauses, then points up to the distant cliff face. "But the best ones involve that obelisk."

You squint up in the direction from which you came. The obelisk is nothing more than a tiny dark finger against the sky.

"Well if you're right, then we need to hurry."

You can continue on through the city by *TURNING TO PAGE 111*

22

The giant jewel sparkles in the torchlight. Waif sets to it with his knife.

"Hey. Um..."

He already has it loose! It's the biggest, most amazing jewel you've ever seen. You step forward to help him...

BOOM!

The wall collapses outward. It knocks Waif to the ground, but then he's swept up in a torrent of rushing water!

"The river!" you exclaim as icy water rapidly fills the room. "The underground aquifer that once fed the ci–"

Your sentence is never finished as your mouth fills with water. It surges into the room, thousands upon thousands of gallons, filling the cave in mere seconds.

"Waif!" Your scream is little more than a gurgle. But it's too late. He's already gone. You try to fight the current, but the river drags you along the cave with unrelenting force. It pins you against the ceiling...

As the water keeps rising, you realize this must be

THE END

Carefully you slide, push and prod certain areas of the green crystal case, being careful with its delicate, four-thousand year old components. Waif looks on in amazement as you make your way through the puzzle box. You might as well be pulling off the greatest magic trick of all time.

At one point you stop. A small silver needle protrudes from one of the slides near the bottom. You ask Waif for his knife, and with the tip of the blade, you pry the needle out and toss it to the sandy floor.

"What was that?" Waif asks.

"Nothing good."

A few more minutes go by. Then, just as you're about to give up and stuff the box into your rucksack...

CLICK!

The crystal box swings open on tiny silver hinges. Inside, resting on a crushed pillow of red velvet, are two snake-sculpted rings of bright yellow gold.

"Pick one," you tell your partner. Reverently Waif chooses the ring with aquamarine eyes. He leaves you the one with eyes of diamond.

"We're ring buddies now," you tell him as you carefully tuck the box into your pack. Waif looks back at you utterly confused.

"Never mind," you smile. "Let's head up and get what we came for."

Not a bad job!

Now climb to the top of the tower by *TURNING TO PAGE 122*

24

"Remember when we saw this constellation before?" you say. "Back in the city square?"

Waif nods.

"It was missing two stars. The second and the fourth." You examine those two gems on the wall. They're both red. Garnets, maybe rubies. "Here, give me your knife."

Using the point of the blade, being very careful not to chip the gems, you pry the jewels loose from the surrounding sandstone. To your surprise, they pop out rather easily. You turn around and hand them to Waif. "Do your thing."

Your friend smiles. Climbing the statue is child's play for him. Waif shimmies up the neck, straddles the head, and places the two gemstone into the serpent's eye sockets. Nothing happens.

"I don't know what–"

Without warning a slab of stone directly in front of the statue grinds to one side. Simultaneously, the snake's head dips down, until its nose is pointing directly at the newly-formed hole.

Waif hops down and shoves his torch into the darkness. Another chamber lies just beneath you, not far down.

"Well I guess that's the way," he shrugs. He hands you the torch, hangs from the lip, and drops down easily into the new room. "Come on, it's all good."

You throw Waif your rucksack and look back at the serpent one last time. And for one brief instant, you'd swear that its eyes glow.

Glad you didn't have to take any of those other corridors? You should be.

Now *HEAD TO PAGE 142*

The top chamber of the Ziggurat is a perfect square. Two tunnels lead into the room from the east and west. Your eyes however are drawn instantly upward, to where a deep red light streams into the dusty chamber.

"The star ruby!"

Nestled against a hole in the ceiling is a breathtaking, fist-sized gemstone. It refracts the sunlight streaming in from above, bathing the entire room in shimmering waves of crimson and scarlet.

"But how do we get to it?" Waif asks. "There's no way up."

He's right. The stone is set into the dead center of the ceiling, a good thirty feet overhead. There's nothing in the chamber to climb on. The only features are two enormous stone blocks, one above either exit, and what looks to be a crude lever next to each. They appear to act as counterweights for some sort of gate or doorway.

"What does your uncle's journal say?"

"*Grand*-uncle," you smirk. You pull it from your rucksack and flip through the timeworn pages. "There's not much here, only a single line. It says: *In Darkness all Will be Revealed.*"

"That doesn't even rhyme." Waif actually sounds disappointed.

You think for a moment, then re-examine the room. It's still very early morning. Sunlight streams in from both exits. Maybe if you closed one...

"We need the room dark," you tell Waif. "Help me close one of these doors."

If you pull the lever on the east side of the chamber *HEAD OVER TO PAGE 120*
Or maybe the lever on the west side would be better. If so, *TURN TO PAGE 148*

26

You stare first at the blue sapphire, then at the red lense. A thought occurs to you.

"Purple."

Waif raises an eyebrow. Striding past him you pick up the red sphere and mount it directly in front of the star jewel. Sunlight passes through the both of them, turning the room a beautiful violet color.

CLICK!

Deep in the floor somewhere, a mechanism activates. The room fills with the loud grinding of stone on stone as the granite door is lifted slowly back into position, clearing your exit. There's another click as it locks into place.

"Purple is the color of *royalty*," you explain to Waif. "Blue and red make purple."

You move to the mosaic and carefully close your palm over the star jewel. It rotates a quarter turn to the left, then pops easily into your hand.

Great job! You just recovered the star sapphire of Atraharsis!

A rumble somewhere off in the distance drags you back to reality. It's nothing like the first tremor, but it's a sobering reminder that your time here is limited.

You wave the big jewel in the air. "If we want to keep this thing we'd better get moving." With that you place the gem securely in your rucksack and lead Waif out of the temple.

Your adventure continues when you *TURN TO PAGE 116*

"We're here to explore the city," you say simply. "Not rush blindly through it."

With that, you step forward to where several broken buildings are marked with a series glyphs and symbols. Very few of them are recognizable. Not even from your grand-uncle's journal.

One however, you manage to translate as a pair of words: *The Serpent.* Above the inscription are a large number of star-shaped dots, all painted in blue. They're arranged in a vaguely snake-like pattern.

You squint at it for a moment, and then it comes to you. "Wait, I know this. This is the Hydra."

"Hydra?"

"Yeah, it's a constellation." A fond memory flashes through your mind; you and your grand-uncle laying in the field behind his manor, staring up at the stars. "Back then I'm sure they called it the serpent, but that's what it is."

Your friend looks at you skeptically. "Are you sure?"

You trace the dots with one finger. "Yeah, totally. The number two and number four stars are missing, but the rest of it is unmistakable."

Waif considers this. "It makes sense I suppose. The founders of Atraharsis were said to have been great astronomers."

"Great engineers, great stonemasons, great astronomers..." You can't help but laugh. "Is there anything these people *weren't* great at?"

"Yes," Waif answers. He scoops up a pile of sand and lets it slip through his fingers. "Longevity."

The rest of the area is empty. Keep on exploring as you *TURN TO PAGE 21*

28

"Gold and red... gold and red..." you repeat the words out loud. "That sound about right to you, Waif?"

Your partner nods. Together you each grab one of the levers, count down from three, and then pull. For a long moment nothing happens. Then a loud grinding causes you to whirl to the right, where a stone door has retracted into the floor.

Warily you head inside. The room is slightly smaller, the walls polished smooth on all sides. An astounding layer of dust covers everything, thicker than anything you've seen so far. It's obvious no one has been in here in... well, forever.

"Oh... wow." Before you know it you're holding Waif's torch. Using only his shirt sleeve, he wipes four thousand years of grime from one of the walls.

You sneeze violently, several times. "What is it?"

Scrawled over the walls, on every side of the room, are a series of elaborate diagrams. Beneath them, etched in perfect detail, is a large scale map of Atraharsis.

"Look here." Waif traces a finger along the wall in several places. "The river originates beneath the cliff face. And these are access points, where water is funneled to different parts of the city. Fountains, wells – here, this one goes all the way up to the obelisk."

Again you sneeze. Through watery eyes, you watch Waif point out many different aspects of the schematics. "Impressive," you tell him. "But does it say anything about the Hall of Kings?"

Waif turns back to the diagrams. As he does, a low rumble shakes the chamber. You both freeze, bracing for a rush of water that never comes. Dust floats down from the ceiling like snow.

"We need to hurry," you say. "We've already been down here way too long."

Backtrack into the machine room and take the shadowy corridor.
TURN TO PAGE 44

With the reflexes of a hockey goalie you reach out and smack Waif's wrist. The scorpion goes flying across the room. It scurries away, ending the danger. But when your friend's arm returns to its prior position, there's a tiny red dot on the back of his hand.

"It stung me." Waif's voice is sad, melancholy. You don't like the sound of it. There's too much resignation.

"Maybe it wasn't poisonous?" you say hopefully.

"No," he tells you calmly. "It was."

You reach for his hand. Maybe if you act fast enough you can squeeze the poison from the wound. But Waif pulls away as if reading your mind. "You can't. It doesn't work like that."

His face goes pale and his knees buckle. You catch him as he falls, but not before Waif knocks over the other two lenses. In slow motion you watch as they shatter against the stone floor of the temple.

With Waif sick, and the two of you trapped in the inner sanctum, you slowly come to the grim realization that this is probably

---

THE END

30

"This place is huge," you say. "There has to be something here."

With that, you and Waif begin searching the library. Since everything is over four thousand years old, most of it falls to ruin at your touch. Some of it has survived though, preserved deep beneath the cool desert sands.

You find few things of interest; some old quills, some decorative tiles, a container that might have once held some sort of ink. But it's under a broken table that you find the most interesting item: a partially intact chest.

"Waif, look at this."

You pull forth a yellowed map of Atraharsis. Most of it has faded into obscurity, but you can still see the near-invisible lines of corridors and hallways running *beneath* the city.

"The catacombs," Waif says. "They were halls carved out by the engineers of Atraharsis, by order of its many kings."

Beneath the map you find a pair of carved jade bookends. They appear very valuable. As you reach for them, Waif's eyes go wide with terror.

"No! Wait!"

Hurry! Roll two dice! (Or just pick a random number from 2 to 12)

If the total is 10 or greater, *TURN TO PAGE 76*

If the total is 9 or less, FLIP DOWN TO PAGE 94

You step forward and kick over the pile of bones. Scattering them away with the toe of your boot, the symbol of a horse is revealed.

"What does it mean?" you ask Waif. Only Waif is long gone. He's already halfway back down the alleyway.

A symbol *beneath* the bones. Hmm...

A clicking sound reaches your ears, from somewhere not far in the distance. You can't pinpoint the direction, but for some reason it sends a shiver right through you.

Best thing to do now is to catch up with Waif. *TURN TO PAGE 102*

32

Your partner's eyes go wide as he heeds your last-second warning. He dives. Then, as you look on in horror, he's buried beneath a ton of sand and rubble.

"Waif!"

You scramble around the monolith, fearing the worst. But when the dust settles you find your friend safe and sound, sprawled out just beyond reach of the falling mountain of rock.

"Thanks," Waif says as you pull him to his feet. "I didn't see it coming down."

Together you haul away the base stones that once made up the bottom of the tower. When you finish clearing away the dust and sand, a third glyph is there. It's a snake.

"Horse, hawk, serpent," you repeat, scrawling them in your grand-uncle's journal. "Bad glyphs."

Waif brushes himself off and looks up at you. "The worst."

Slip that journal back in your rucksack and *TURN TO PAGE 41*

The sand-strewn road winds its way north and east, past several broken tenements and shattered homes. The architecture of Atraharsis is inherently beautiful. Even in its ruined state, you can make out the pride with which everything here was once built and maintained.

All of a sudden Waif stops. His face is drawn with discomfort.

"What is it?"

Your partner looks like he swallowed an onion. "It's nothing," he mutters. "Let's go." He continues walking again, but you notice he's shifted to the other side of the street.

Standing near the road, in the place Waif avoided, is a small mausoleum. The squarely-built tomb is decorated with beautiful columns and cornices. The doors and windows are gone, but tiny shards of colored glass still jut upward from within the frame. What may have once been a statue is broken off at the base.

"Should we check it out?" you ask. Waif cringes visibly. He shoots you a look of dread and dismay.

"Come on," you tell him. "We can't just pass everything by because you're superstitious about it."

If you'd like to explore the mausoleum, *HEAD OVER TO PAGE 86*

If you're pretty sure Waif would faint if you did, skip it and:
Continue along the wider avenue by *TURNING TO PAGE 43*
Or take the side road that veers to the right *OVER ON TO PAGE 97*

34

"Snake eats rodent," you say, picking up the stone embossed with the serpent. You slide it into the center spot.

"And owl eats snake," Waif chimes in. He places the owl stone into the remaining slot, completing the sequence.

For several moments, nothing happens. Then, with a low rumble, the sleek marble column begins retracting into the floor. It happens smoothly, flawlessly. You can only imagine the engineering it took for something like this to work, much less hold up after so many long and buried centuries.

Eventually the column is no more than a pedestal, three feet high. The rumbling stops, and your prize is finally set before you. Waif looks at you expectantly.

"Should... should we just..."

You reach out and remove the beautiful green jewel from its stone mount. The star inside the gemstone reflects back the white brilliance of the sun.

Amazing job! You just recovered the star emerald of Atraharsis!

It's a powerful moment in your life, and you can't help but get choked up about it. You think of all the things you can do now. All of your problems solved...

"My uncle would've loved to have been here," you say sadly.

"*Grand*-uncle," Waif corrects you with a mischievous wink.

The walk back down the tower steps is a lot nicer than the walk up!
Continue on by *TURNING TO PAGE 116*

"Waif, use the torch!"

You point to the moldering pile of tapestries. They're caked with long centuries of dust and filth, but you're crossing your fingers they're still very flammable.

Your partner backs up to the pile. Glancing back to make sure you're clear, he puts the torch to them. The entire heap of fabric erupts in a blaze of yellow flame!

The slug rears back, more from the heat than anything else. Living down here its entire existence, you're fairly sure the creature must be blind. The blaze perfectly illuminates the entire chamber. For now it drives the slug to the opposite end of the cave, but you know it won't last forever. When the pile burns out...

"Look!"

Waif points to an exit – a pitch-black tunnel, not far from where you're standing. It's too small for the slug to get through. You breathe a long, shuddering sigh of relief, and then you're sprinting through the opening. Running side by side along the corridor...

The darkness can't last forever, can it? Find out when you *GO TO PAGE 44*

36

"Let's skirt around the city and head for the East Gate," you say. "It'll give us a better idea of what we're facing."

You walk along hard-packed ground on what was once a well-traveled road. To your left, the sun-bleached, broken walls of the city tower over you. On your right, the desert stretches all the way to the featureless horizon.

For a long while, nothing is out of the ordinary. But then, out of the corner of your eye, you swear you detect a hint of movement somewhere high on the parapets.

Before you can even say anything, Waif starts moving in that direction. "I think I see a crack in the rubble," he explains. "A way into the city."

You frown. "It might be better to stick to the road. We don't even know where the gate is yet."

If you'd like to try Waif's shortcut into Atraharsis, *TURN TO PAGE 134*

If you'd rather continue along the road that leads to the East Gate, *HEAD DOWN TO PAGE 133*

Your eyes fall on the yellow sphere. It gleams a golden color, even in the blue light.

"Gold is royal, isn't it?" You're only thinking aloud now. When Waif says nothing you pick up the yellow lense and mount it directly in front of the blue sapphire. The light shines through the both of them, turning the entire room a sickly green.

The silence is broken by a loud hissing sound. *Snakes!* You spin out in a circle, bracing for an attack that never comes. Nothing else enters the room. Nothing except...

A cloud swirls through the chamber, threatening to envelop you both. Glancing around you notice that up near the ceiling, several stones have retracted into the wall. Spraying forth from these new openings is a shimmering, glimmering cloud of dust. Diamond dust.

"Cover your mouth!" you warn. "Don't breathe it in!"

Roll two dice (or just pick a random number from 2 to 12).

If the total is a 5 or greater, *GO TO PAGE 54*

If the roll comes up a 1, 2, 3, or 4, *FLIP BACK TO PAGE 14*

38

It's no use! No matter how hard you run, the jackals run faster. They've got more legs. More endurance. More–

"Aarrghh!"

Waif screams as one of the creature's teeth tears into his calf. Enough is enough! You stop instantly and move to stand guard over your fallen friend. If they want to get to him they'll have to get through you first!

Between Waif's torch and you screaming your head off, you manage to keep the jackals at bay. Eventually they get tired of trying to find an opening. Slinking away, they head back down the avenue to find easier prey.

"Thank you," Waif says through gritted teeth. You can see he's in obvious pain, clutching his leg tightly with both hands. Gently you pry his fingers away from the wound.

"It's bad," you tell him. "I can stop the bleeding, but you need a doctor. Pronto."

Waif nods, grateful for the help. The good news is you'll both be okay. But your adventure, unfortunately, has to be cut short.

It's a shame, but for now this is

THE END

You mark off a pretty good distance. Then you take a running start, keep your eye on the gap, and at the very last moment, jump...

Only you don't jump. You trip!

You're focusing so much on your footwork that your eyes and body betray each other. Half a meter before the jump you realize your front foot is going to come down too far forward. You try to make a last minute adjustment but your heel slips off the edge of the chasm. Tumbling wildly, you fall backward into the hole!

Waif cries out for you. The sunlight disappears. The last thing you remember is a growing darkness as you fall and fall and fall...

Sorry to say it, but you have reached

THE END

40

"There," you say. "She's pointing to that alley."

Directly in line with the statue's outstretched arm is a narrow avenue. Waif looks at you skeptically for a moment, but still falls in behind you.

The alley is empty, nondescript. Other than sand, it contains nothing. As you continue along, the buildings seem to creep closer in on both sides. The feeling of claustrophobia is unsettling. Then, just as you're about to turn back, the avenue comes to a dead end.

"Ugh."

Against the far wall is a thick pile of bleached bones. They look to have come from a large animal, maybe a camel or something similar. An ominous feeling steals over you, and for some reason you feel wracked with a shudder of despair. You jump at the squawk of a bird of prey, somewhere high overhead.

"This is wrong," Waif says. "We should not be here." He makes a sign in the air, presumably to ward off evil.

If you're brave enough you can search the bones by *TURNING TO PAGE 31*

Then again, no one will blame you for backing out of the alley *OVER ON PAGE 102*

After walking some more you stumble upon a wide area where many streets come together. Several stone pillars form a ring around a central depression, and inside you can easily see the remains of a large fire. The blackened timbers and thousand-year old ashes are mixed in amongst the desert sands.

Leaning against one of the pillars, standing exceptionally tall, is the outline of a human figure. Wordlessly you extend your arm to keep Waif from walking past you.

"Do you think it could be one of your former group?" you whisper. The two of you are crouched down beside a broken hunk of granite.

Your friend shakes his head. "I know all of Sullivan's crew. I've never seen a man that tall."

His words are a relief, but at the same time they create even more mystery. Who could this be? Is he hostile? Dangerous? Above everything else, how did he get here?

"I can probably circle around," you tell Waif, "and get behind him."

"What will you do then?"

You shrug. "Haven't figured that out yet."

The figure is still leaning against the pillar. What's next?

If you decide to circle around and sneak up on the unknown figure *HEAD ON BACK TO PAGE 16*

Or maybe you'd like to take a more direct approach and just call out to him. If so, *FLIP TO PAGE 101*

42

Slowly you step beside Waif, not taking your eyes from the cheetah even for a second. Your hand closes over his as you gently take the torch.

"When I do this," you tell him, "run out of here and don't look back."

Waif looks frozen by fear. You have to tell him two more times before he delivers the smallest, most imperceptible of all nods. Then, fighting against every last ounce of flight instinct, you take a step *toward* the big desert cat.

"HI-YAAAA!!!" you scream, for lack of anything else to say. In one hand you still hold Murdoch's journeyman's pack. With the other, you swing the firebrand before you in a wide, threatening arc.

The cat arches its back... but it retreats. First one step, then two. You scream again, a third time, and by the fourth you're already running full speed, following Waif out of the cave. You're a good hundred yards into the sunlight before you finally stop. Even then you expect to look back and find the creature mid-leap, ready to deliver the killing blow...

"She's gone," Waif assures you. He's right. The road is between you and the cave mouth is totally clear.

Smiling broadly, you hand the torch back and begin rifling through Murdoch's pack. Beyond an empty canteen, a container of lamp oil, and what looks to be some kind of hundred year-old jerky, you find two crumpled, yellowed pages. They have a ragged edge, as if torn from...

"The journal!" you cry. "These are the two missing pages!"

Quickly you open your grand-uncle's journal and match the torn edges to where they were ripped from the book. For the first time in a century, Murdoch's work is once again complete. The pages themselves show only two large glyphs. One is a hawk, the other a snake. Both of the drawings have been crossed out.

"What's it mean?" Waif asks.

"Not sure. But these glyphs are crossed out for a reason."

Solid job. Head down the road some more by *TURNING TO PAGE 97*

The road spills out into an enormous city square. This was a place where crowds would gather to meet, shop, or socialize. You can only imagine what that looked like – thousands of people buying, selling and trading from all manner of distant lands.

All that's left of the place now is sand and silence. Flat, smooth cobbles stretch out in every lonely direction.

"Where to?" Waif asks. You answer him by pointing. The Queen's Tower is now twice as big as it was before. You're getting close.

The road takes you beneath a series of broken archways, back into the streets at the other end of the square. Three rusty iron cages hang from the last arch. Waif mutters a curse and traces a mark in the air with two fingers; a sign of warding.

"This was a place of suffering," he says in disgust.

"Not anymore," you assure him. The cages are empty now, but you'd rather not think of the things they've seen.

A shadow suddenly passes over you, from somewhere high above. It sends an involuntary shudder through your body.

"There are markings up ahead," you say. "Maybe we should check them out."

Waif wholeheartedly disagrees. "No. We should leave this place quickly, and not look back."

If you take the time to check out the markings, *FLIP BACK TO PAGE 27*
If you'd rather take Waif's advice and hurry through this area, *GO TO PAGE 91*

44

You stumble on, shivering against the darkness. With all the past weeks' heat, sweat, and toil, you never once thought you'd be missing the desert sun.

"There's a light on up ahead," Waif says skeptically. He sounds like he only half believes it. "It's... some kind of room."

Sure enough he's right. As your eyes begin readjusting you can start to see things beyond the light of your partner's torch. You emerge from the hallway into a large granite chamber. Tiny shafts cut into the ceiling bring light down here, presumably from somewhere up in the city above.

"Look!"

There's an alcove on the far wall. Recessed within it is a three-pronged dais. Each of the prongs ends in a fist-sized depression, exactly the size and shape of a star jewel.

"I think we're supposed to put our jewel in the right place here," Waif points at the dais.

You don't like the sound of that one bit. "Are you sure?"

"Well, no. But there's nothing else in the whole room."

You walk the entire chamber just to make sure. Nothing else. No other exits. Just Waif, you, the dais, and the star gemstone resting snugly in your rucksack. You pull it out with a heavy sigh. Hold it in your palm one last time...

Which star jewel did you recover? Use the chart below to add up all the letters in that word. Once you have the total, you can TURN TO THAT PAGE.

A = 1	F = 6	K = 11	P = 16	U = 21	Z = 26
B = 2	G = 7	L = 12	Q = 17	V = 22	Example:
C = 3	H = 8	M = 13	R = 18	W = 23	OPAL =
D = 4	I = 9	N = 14	S = 19	X = 24	15+16+1+12
E = 5	J = 10	O = 15	T = 20	Y = 25	= 44

Do you have the star RUBY?

Did you obtain the star EMERALD?

Or maybe you recovered the star SAPPHIRE?

You're out time. Out of room! As much as you hate the idea of making the attempt, the floor retracts more with every second that goes by.

Flattening yourself against the wall, you take three lunging steps. On the fourth one you jump...

But the distance is too far.

Even with Waif reaching out for you, you fall woefully short of the other hallway. Your arms pinwheel through the air as you drop helplessly into the cold, dark waters of the raging river.

Oh, man! You came so close!

Not for a lack of trying, but this is obviously

THE END

46

When Waif lit the fires, the floor started moving. Maybe putting them out will stop it.

"Douse the braziers!"

Waif grabs his canteen while you pull yours from your rucksack. Upending them onto the coals, you put both fires out in no time. But nothing happens! The chamber grows dark again. The ceiling is sickeningly close.

Death by Fire...

"Quick, light them again!" you cry. "Light them so we can search the room for another way!"

But it's no use. The coals are much too wet now. As you struggle for an answer the room grows smaller. Darker. Waif's torch goes out, and that's when you realize this must be

THE END

With your arm outstretched you begin to rotate the key to the right. There's a sharp click, and then you step back as the entire obelisk begins to turn on its own. It goes through all four faces, turning a full 360 degrees with the loud grinding of stone on stone. Then it stops, and everything goes silent. The obelisk key pops back out and drops into your hand.

"That was weird," Waif says. "I don't know what–"

Without warning you feel the ground shift beneath you. There's a tremendous crack – like the biggest thunderclap you ever heard, but somewhere muffled and very far away. The noise is followed by what sounds like rushing water. It gets louder. Closer. Just in front of you, a tremendous field of dust begins rising into the air.

"The ground's falling away!"

You grab Waif and pull him down, kneeling against the obelisk for what little protection it brings. Right before your eyes, the desert floor drops away. What you thought was water was actually sand; millions of tons of it drop off into what seems like an endless, bottomless pit. The sinkhole expands outward in a geometric progression. Thankfully, it's moving away from you.

"Cover your mouth!" Waif shouts. "And your eyes!"

You mimic your new friend by pulling your shirt over your face. You can't see. You can't hear. Your ears are filled with television static, a thousand times louder than anything you've ever heard in your life. Eventually the ground stops shaking and the sound drops down to a low hiss. When the dust finally settles you find yourself standing at the top of a sheer cliff wall. Hundreds of feet down, the ancient, broken ruins of a city lays sprawled out beneath you.

You found it!

48

"Atraharsis!" you roar. "There it is!"

The once-great city of Kings is breathtaking, even in its ruined state. Atraharsis's walls barely stand. Its temples and palaces are a crumbled ruin, blocks of stone and masonry scattered like hundreds of yellowed dice. Even as you watch, more sand drains away. Piles of it still line the cobbled streets, but for the most part the city is revealed.

"It was here the whole time," you swear. You still can't believe it. "Right beneath us."

"The City Beneath the Sands," Waif says. "It was always said."

A jagged path zigs and zags its way downward from the obelisk. You follow along, being careful not to trip over any rubble that could put you over the edge. It's still a long way down. Waif stays right with you, picking his way along the narrow ledge. He's having a much easier time of it than you are.

The path winds its way westward, skirting the edge of the city. When it finally spits you out, you stand before a broken opening in the enormous city walls.

"This is the Great Gate," you tell Waif. "Murdoch's journal has a crude map. Hang on..." You reach into your rucksack. "Ah, here it is."

Cliff Face

Pavilion

Queen's Tower

Grand Plaza

Necropolis

Temple of Luus'

The Ziggurat

Ruins?

East Gate

Great Gate

Atraharsis
City Beneath the Sands

50

"It was known as the *Grand* Gate," Waif tells you. "Your map has it wrong."

You look back at the city and shrug. There's nothing great *or* grand about the opening in the wall. In fact there's not even a gate anymore, if there even was one to begin with. Written on the back side of the map is another message. You read it out loud:

Three Star Jewels, Three Deadly Trials
Before the Walls Will Sing
It Takes Nine Lives
From Six Less Five
To Find the Hall of Kings

"Well we only have two lives," Waif says. "So that may be a problem." He studies the map for a moment. "Your map shows the location of the star jewels," he says with interest. "Sullivan's map wasn't nearly as detailed."

The jewels stare back at you seductively, beckoning you as they did your grand-uncle. Even one of them would be enough to live the rest of your days in comfort. Not to mention Atraharsis's other hidden treasures, plus the fabled riches supposedly buried in the secret chamber known as the Hall of Kings.

"Waif listen," you begin. "You need a boss. I need a crew. As of right now, you're hired. If you want the job, that is."

For a moment all your friend does is stare up at the yellowed walls of the ancient city. Then he smiles. The sun gleams off a pair of golden teeth. "I'm in." He extends one calloused hand in your direction and you shake it.

"Okay Mr. Young–"

"Donovan."

"Okay *Donovan*," Waif says with a slight bow. "Where do we begin?"

Your map shows two potential entrances to the city of Atraharsis. Only one of them is visible.

If you decide to head in through the Great/Grand Gate, *TURN TO PAGE 109*

If you'd rather skirt the city and look for the East Gate, *TURN TO PAGE 36*

You walk for minutes that seem like hours in the darkness. Waif leads with the torch held out before him, turning left and right with vague purpose. You hear nothing. See nothing. This makes it all the more nerve-wracking, because you expect the worst at any moment.

"There's a room here," Waif says.

Up ahead, the corridor widens into a large chamber. The torchlight illuminates everything, including the walls. All of it is bare. There's nothing anywhere, except–

"Look! The floor!"

Directly beneath your feet, a complete map of Atraharsis has been meticulously painted from wall to wall. It includes everything, from the Ziggurat to the Temple to the Queen's Tower. The colors haven't faded much, even after all this time. The overall attention to detail is incredible.

Waif points. "See these lines?" In a lighter ink, another schematic has been laid over the map itself. "These are the Underhalls. The very catacombs we're in right now. They stretch beneath the city, and–"

A blue vein follows beneath the cliff face on the map. It shoots off in several directions, along streets and avenues, including a wide vein that flows up through the cliff itself. There, at the top, is an unmistakable drawing of the obelisk.

"The aquifer!" Waif cries. "The one that feeds the oasis! See how it runs beneath the city? Through to the pools, the fountains," his finger traces upward, "and then to the obelisk itself!"

"So?"

"This is how the engineers hid the city! When Atraharsis became threatened they channeled the river, running the waters beneath these halls to sink the city beneath the sands!"

The thought of millions of gallons of water rushing beneath you is more than a bit disquieting. Still, the knowledge it took to build this place...

"Come on," you say. "Let's not give this city a reason to keep us."

Better keep moving. *TURN TO PAGE 152*

52

The slug bears down on you. It's just too big. The torch is too small. You're out of options. Unless...

"Waif!" you shout. "Throw me your pack!"

He does. You flip it open, reach inside, and pull out a giant fistful of the pink rock salt.

You throw it.

The salt strikes the slug with exactly the desired reaction. It recoils in pain, halting its advance and rearing back in confusion.

"It's working!" Waif yells.

You grab another handful of salt, then another, spreading it out a wide arc. Soon the slug is twisting and writhing on the far side of the cavern. No longer a threat, you stop.

"Find us an exit," you tell Waif. "Hurry."

Using the torch, your partner works his way along the wall. You keep one hand in Waif's bag, your eyes on the slug. All the fight has gone out of it. You're pretty sure you'll be okay when–

"Found one," Waif calls. "Over here."

A pitch-black opening is cut roughly into one wall. It's the only way out of the room.

"Let's go," you tell Waif as you hand back his pack. There's hardly any salt left. He looks crushed.

"Yeah, sorry about that."

Continue along the pitch-black tunnel when you *TURN TO PAGE 44*

54

You follow the growing cloud back to its origins. Up near the ceiling, several stone blocks have retracted into the wall. The diamond dust pouring out from them has already stopped. All you have to do now is ride it out.

"Close your eyes!" you shout as it washes over you. "Don't blink!"

For several moments you do nothing but stand there, eyes squinted shut, breathing as shallowly as possible through the collar of your shirt. You can only hope that Waif heard you in time.

Eventually, the dust settles. You give it another minute or two to be safe, then carefully peek out from beneath your shirt. Waif is doing exactly the same thing. He's okay!

You pull the yellow lense from the mount and replace it on the dais.

"We need a better choice," you tell Waif. You hold up the other two lenses. "Which one?"

If you try the red lense *HEAD TO PAGE 26*
If you go with the green lense, *TURN TO PAGE 74*

The street widens here, the sand pushed back to reveal a great cobbled avenue with structures on both sides. Everything is shattered beyond recognition. You close your eyes and try to imagine Atraharsis as it once was, picturesque and beautiful, boasting the world's greatest engineers and some of the most advanced architecture of its time.

"This was a city of peace," you say. "Or at least, that's what my grand-uncle used to tell me."

Waif nods. "Peace and knowledge. Somehow the kings and queens of Atraharsis avoided war. At one point it was the center of all trade; a sparkling jewel in the heart of the desert, fed from beneath by the waters of a great spring."

Your foot catches on yet another mound of dust. It's hard for you to imagine this city ever had water. It's the driest, most sun-scorched place you've ever seen.

"And one more thing," Waif adds. "I was thinking–"

The ground beneath you abruptly gives way. The sensation of falling ends in a violent landing, all the breath knocked from your lungs. You throw your arms up as broken cobbles rain down all around you.

When the dust finally settles you're in a basement of chiseled sandstone. A pitch black tunnel yawns to your right. That's when you notice the chattering. Dozens of enormous rats have encircled you. Noses sniffing the air, they squint upward as if they've never seen the sun. Slowly they begin to close in...

"Wait!" Waif cries. "Don't move!"

Don't move? Is he *kidding* you?

There's probably just enough time to take the pitch black tunnel. You can do that by *GOING TO PAGE 110*

On the other hand, Waif *did* tell you not to move. If you decide to stay still, *TURN TO PAGE 75*

56

"Quick, get behind these rocks!" you shout. "While there's still time!"

With a nimbleness you only wish you possessed, Waif vaults over the stones behind you. He's already disappeared from view by the time you finish your own mad scramble.

The lizard stomps over to where you're hiding. Craning its neck, it leans down and lifts up one of the stones in its tremendous maw.

"It's trying to find us!" you warn your friend. "We have to get to another–"

"No," Waif tells you firmly. "Look."

You glance up to find the monster no longer coming. In fact, it's now taking the smooth white stone back in the direction it came.

"We woke it up," Waif explains, "when we first raised the city. But it's not after us. It's after its eggs."

You reach back and rap your knuckles against one of the broken pillars. "But these are just rocks."

Waif shrugs. "It doesn't know that. Yet."

You watch the big lizard as it disappears down the next street. Fortunately it's not moving in the direction you need to go.

"Come on," you tell your partner. "The tower is just up ahead."

The Queen's Tower awaits! *FLIP DOWN TO PAGE 111*

"Run!"

You turn on your heels and sprint, willing your feet to move faster than you've ever run in your life. All you can do is move forward. There's no time to look back, no time to worry about whether or not Waif is still with you. All that exists, right now at least, are your feet and the road.

After a while the exertion takes its toll. Sweat beads along your face and neck. It runs into your eyes, stinging like crazy.

"Waif?" you call back blindly. A grunt over your shoulder tells you he's still there. But you can hear the dogs too, and you're not entirely sure you can outrun them.

Roll a single die (or just pick a random number from 1 to 6).

If the roll is a 1, 2, 3, or 5, *GO TO PAGE 118*

If the roll comes up as a 4 or 6, *FLIP OVER TO PAGE 38*

58

You set the star emerald in its position on the dais. A noise startles you from above, and you jump back...

Three enormous stone columns fall from the ceiling. They slam into the floor right where you were standing, creating a thick stone portcullis that cuts you off from the alcove!

"Over there!" Waif shouts. Off to your left, a door is sliding open. You ignore it for the moment and reach between the stone columns. Your arm goes through... then your shoulder. But the gap is too small. The emerald gleams in the shadows, tantalizingly just beyond your reach.

"It's closing!"

Waif's right. The door is sliding in the other direction now, once again becoming part of the wall. There isn't any time...

"Come on," you say reluctantly. "We have to go!"

The door is half closed by the time you slide into the darkened hallway. But Waif isn't there. You call back for him as the seconds tick by. The opening becomes a narrow sliver of light, separating you from the darkness.

"Waif!"

At the last possible second, he slips through. The door slams shut behind him. The torch flickers wildly as a small corridor is revealed.

"Where do you think it leads?" your partner asks.

"I don't know." You look back forlornly in the direction of your beautiful lost emerald. "But it had better be worth it."

The corridor deposits you into a long stone chamber. Three exits are spaced equidistant from each other at the opposite end. In the center, mounted on a smooth platform, is the magnificently-carved statue of a giant serpent.

"Is this the Hall of Kings?" Waif asks. "Doesn't seem very... kingly."

Three of the walls here are featureless stone. The fourth however, is studded with multi-colored gemstones in a long trailing pattern. Sort of like...

"The Hydra."

Your partner squints. "The constellation?"

"Yes. See how the jewels are spaced?" You trace a line from point to point. "Seventeen stars. Seventeen gemstones." Looking back at the statue, you notice it follows the same serpentine shape. But the sculpture has no adornment at all.

Waif bends over the platform, where a small series of glyphs have been etched into the side. "The serpent sees the way," he translates. "Doesn't make much sense. The statue couldn't see if it wanted to – its eyes are missing."

You follow his gaze to the snake's head. Two holes are carved where the eyes would be. Holes exactly the same size and shape as–

"The gems!" you cry. "Waif, we need to put the statue's eyes back!" You look at the wall. The constellation's line of colorful jewels shimmers like liquid in the torchlight.

"Sounds about right," Waif agrees. "But which ones?"

If you *know* which two jewels to use (and don't guess!) take those two numbers and then *GO TO THAT PAGE*

(For example, if you think it's the 5th jewel and the 9th jewel you would go to page 59). Once again, don't guess!

If you have no idea which jewels to pick, you'll have to choose one of the three exits and hope for the best!

To take the hallway on the left, *TURN TO PAGE 155*

To take the hallway on the right, *GO TO PAGE 68*

To take the center hallway, *HEAD OVER TO PAGE 149*

60

"Water!" you think quickly. "Give me your canteen!"

Waif has his canteen unslung in seconds. You uncap it and begin pouring, watching as the water flows in through the top of the altar and out through the many holes on all sides.

Nothing happens.

Maybe it's not enough, you think. Reaching into your rucksack you produce your own canteen. You empty it into the altar, watching as it too dribbles out the sides. The result is the same: the floor still grinds inevitably upward.

Waif looks at you with fear in his eyes. "Try something else!"

Put out the braziers' flames by *TURNING TO PAGE 46*

You could also try pouring sand into the altar *OVER ON PAGE 151*

Fingers crossed, eyes closed, you step on a black tile. Long seconds tick by... Nothing happens.

Slowly you shift forward, adding more and more weight until you're totally committed. Finally, you're standing on it. Waif lets out a long, strained sigh.

"Good choice."

You glance down for the next black tile, it's simply too far away. You'll need to step on one of the other colors first...

Without hesitating you pick red. Again you move slowly, carefully, shifting your body weight until the red tile fully supports you. Again, you're safe.

"Avoid the white ones," you call back to your partner. You can hear him begin moving behind you. Together you make your way down the hall, being extremely careful not to touch any of the light-colored tiles. When the floor turns back to flagstone at the very end, you're both relieved.

Waif holds his torch back for one last look. "What do you think would've happened if–"

"Don't know," you say. "Don't care."

The tunnel ahead is pitch-black. Continue along it by *TURNING TO PAGE 44*

62

"Waif, help! I can't–"

You let go. You don't think about it, it just happens. Your fingers aren't strong enough to grip the rock one-handed. As they give way you close your eyes and brace yourself for that sickening, falling sensation reserved only for the worst possible nightmares...

But the feeling never comes. When you open your eyes again Waif has you by the wrist. His face is red from the strain of holding your weight. Grabbing him with your free hand, you swing your leg up and catch your foot on the next ledge. You pull yourself onto the stone platform, your chest still heaving.

"Thanks for that," you gasp once you catch your breath. "I thought for sure that was it."

Waif smiles and helps you to your feet. "No more climbing for you," he quips. He offers you some water from his canteen, and the two of you continue onward.

You made it! Barely. Good job anyway. *FLIP BACK TO PAGE 25*

The ground shakes. The air fills with dust. The wall comes down...

CRASH!

Pain spikes up your leg as a heavy piece of stone strikes your ankle. You yank your leg in, trying to stay as small a target as possible until the whole thing is over. Eventually the tremors stop. Everything goes still, and the dust begins to settle.

Waif comes running over, his face painted with concern. "Are you okay?"

You pull up your pants leg and start rubbing your ankle. At least there's no cut or laceration.

"Could be broken, could be sprained," you say. "Impossible to tell. Here, help me up."

With Waif's aid, you get back to your feet. Your ankle takes your body's weight with little problem. That's a good thing.

"I think I'm okay," you tell your friend. "Whatever it is, there's not an X-ray machine for hundreds of miles anyway. We have a few hours before the whole thing swells up, so let's not waste them."

You didn't think you'd get through this thing without a couple of bumps and bruises, did you?

Continue deeper into the city by *TURNING TO PAGE 105*

64

The sinkhole is still expanding. Leaving solid ground now would be a foolish move, and it probably wouldn't help your friend one bit. You have to think...

Quickly you reach down and grab Waif's own pack. Just inside the leather flap is a coil of rope!

"Here!" you shout down to him. "Grab it!"

You fling one end of the rope toward him, but Waif is still sliding. There's a blind panic in his eyes. Luckily, he has just enough presence of mind to heed you. He lunges for the rope with both hands, catching it only barely with his right.

You brace one foot against the nearest piece of granite and then you pull hard. Slowly, Waif emerges from the sands. First his shoulders, then his arms, then his waist are free. By the time his knees show, your partner is crawling his way up to the edge of the sinkhole.

Eventually the sand-slide stops. You lie flat on your backs for a moment, the both of you breathing heavy, staring up into the early morning sky.

"Thanks," Waif says when he can speak again.

You hold up his rope. "Thank *this*."

Whew, close call! The sinkhole blocks any chance of entering the city through Waif's shortcut.

You can keep on toward the East Gate (staying on the path this time!) by *TURNING TO PAGE 133*

Or you can turn back and head to the Great Gate by *GOING TO PAGE 109*

You follow the passage to the north, where it descends deeper into the desert earth. The air is colder here. A chill runs through you as the sweat of your prior exertion in the city begins to cool on your skin.

"It keeps going down," Waif notes. "And look at the walls."

The smooth paved stones give way to rough cut walls of pure sandstone. You see tool marks everywhere.

"This was their quarry," you say. "They took stone from down here to build up Atraharsis."

"Wouldn't that weaken the city's foundation?" Waif asks.

"I don't know. I'm not an engineer."

A distant roar reaches your ears as the passage widens into a system of caves. The roar grows louder as you approach the far wall. The wall is damp! It's even weeping in some places. In others, the light from Waif's torch glints off a few stones embedded into the walls.

"Gems!" Waif runs his hand over a few of the larger stones. The clarity is stunning. Pulling his knife, Waif pries loose one of the pale blue stones. It takes up most of his palm, reflecting beautifully in the light of his torch.

"This place is a mine!" he cries. He scans the wall and points at a tremendous gem, almost as large as his head. "Look at that! We're rich!"

You take a hesitant step forward. "Yeah..." Half of you is thrilled. The other half is not so happy about the amount of water seeping out of the wall. Especially in places where the wall is cracked, and around some of the gemstones.

"Come on," Waif says. He sets the torch down temporarily. "Help me with this big one."

If you'd like to be filthy rich, help Waif pry loose the big jewel *OVER ON PAGE 22*

Or maybe you should continue on. If that's your choice, *FLIP DOWN TO PAGE 89*

66

You place the star ruby on the dais.

"Look out!"

Waif yanks you backward as three large stone columns slam down from the ceiling. Little more than a foot apart they act as a crude stone portcullis, cutting you off from the alcove. Your gemstone gleams red behind them, even in the shadows.

"Maybe we can..."

There's the familiar noise of stone on stone as a door grinds open somewhere behind you. Numbly you watch as it slides all the way to one side, clicks loudly, and immediately begins closing again.

"Waif, come on!" Anxiously you step into the shadows of the new corridor. When you turn back, Waif is still back at the portcullis, agonizing over the star jewel. The door is still closing... "WAIF!"

He's not going to make it. As the door all but seals the passageway, you scramble helplessly for something to prop it open. There's nothing around!

BOOM!

The door closes. But at the last possible second... Waif slides through. He does it sideways, with almost superhuman speed, his shirt tearing up the back as it gets caught between several tons of grinding sandstone. The torch flickers wildly in the darkness.

"That was foolish," you chide your friend. "You almost became a permanent feature."

Waif nods, still shaken. When he's finally okay you keep moving.

Up ahead the small corridor ends, opening in another area. The torchlight reveals a perfectly round chamber with an exit at the opposite end. It's entirely empty and nondescript, except for one thing:

"What's that sound?"

An odd, background noise fills your ears. It's more of a buzzing, or maybe a rushing sound. As you enter the room, it seems to originate from every direction at once.

"Where's it coming from?" you ask. "The walls?"

Waif tilts his head. "No, I don't think so." He approaches the opposite hallway. "Perhaps there's–"

The two of you are jarred instantly off your feet. One knee explodes with pain as you go down, and it's not until you stand up again that you realize–

"The floor is moving!"

The grinding of stone against stone is drowned out by an almost deafening roar. The air is suddenly alive, swirling with a cool wind and... moisture? Waif is pointing. Shouting. You can barely hear him. "The river!"

You look down, over the edge of the retracting floor which is already halfway gone. Beneath you, not far down, a portion of the underground river thunders past. It's loud, powerful. It sounds like the end of the world.

As the floor continues its disappearing act you're forced against one wall. Set into into stone, you notice something you didn't before: a small, diamond-shaped depression. *A key goes here...* you realize.

On the opposite end of the chamber, Waif's already made the deadly jump for the other exit. As usual, he made it. But it looks far too long a jump for you...

Do you have an object that would fit in the diamond-shaped hole? If so, use the chart below to add up all the letters in that word. Once you have the total, you can *GO TO THAT PAGE*

A = 1	F = 6	K = 11	P = 16	U = 21	Z = 26
B = 2	G = 7	L = 12	Q = 17	V = 22	Example:
C = 3	H = 8	M = 13	R = 18	W = 23	ANNA =
D = 4	I = 9	N = 14	S = 19	X = 24	1+14+14+1
E = 5	J = 10	O = 15	T = 20	Y = 25	= 30

If you don't have anything, you'll just have to jump! Roll two dice (or just pick a random number from 2 to 12).

If you roll an ODD number, *TURN TO PAGE 144*
If you roll an EVEN number, *TURN TO PAGE 45*

68

You've no idea which gemstones to pry from the constellation. Rather than chance being wrong, you walk to the other end of the room.

"Pick an exit," you tell Waif. It seems like a good idea. So far your friend hasn't steered you wrong.

Waif peers into each of the three openings with the torch. "They all look the same," he shrugs. "Let's go right."

A minute later you're pretty far down the long corridor when it abruptly dead-ends.

"Hmm..." Waif says. "Maybe if we–" he stops. "Wait, did you just hear a click?"

"No. Nothing."

BOOM!

A solid block of granite explodes from the ceiling behind you, neatly sealing the corridor. It's big and thick and totally impenetrable. It must weigh several dozen tons.

You wait, half expecting another door to open... but nothing more happens. You're boxed in, surrounded by stone on all four sides. There's nothing to look at. Nothing to see. And they'll be even less, you're afraid, when Waif's torch finally goes out.

"Maybe someone will come," Waif offers. "Sullivan's crew, or perhaps someone else. Maybe if we shouted *really* loud..."

Fear grips you in the darkness. It's an awful lot of 'maybes'.

All you can do is cross your fingers and hope for the best. But for now at least, this is

---

THE END

You stand before the remains of a once-magnificent palace. The sport carvings and mosaics, and the floors are set with tiles of jade, jet, and lapis. There were probably tapestries and rugs as well, but these are long gone. Victims of time, the elements, and the desert sands.

Waif stands beside you as explore the residence's broken halls. He drops back slowly, however, as a distant sound picks up.

Somewhere ahead, you hear low moaning. It rises and falls with the wind, at times sounding like someone is in excruciating pain. Waif mutters something unintelligible and traces a sign of warding in the air with one hand. As you turn the next corner, the source of the noise comes into view.

It's a face. Set against the far wall is the large ceramic visage of a bearded man. His expression is twisted, his lips pursed together in what could be either a tight grin or a frown, depending on what angle you look from.

"Let's check it out," you say. But Waif is already a half dozen steps behind you. Whatever you're going to do here, it's obvious you'll do it alone.

If you continue to search the rest of the ruined palace before continuing, *GO TO PAGE 132*

Or maybe it would be safer to just head back to the street. If that's your decision, *TURN TO PAGE 55*

J

You act without thinking. With one hand you shove Waif out of the way. With your other, you grab his torch.

The spider misses your friend by mere inches. It lands, turns, and begins scurrying straight in Waif's direction. Sweeping your arm downward, you set the torch to it. The creature rears back as it catches fire and begins screeching like a wounded animal.

You help Waif to his feet, being sure to hold the torch out in front of you to ward off another attack. Instead the spider scampers backward and buries itself beneath a pile of sand.

"Did– did you see the markings on its back?" Waif gasps. "That creature was deadly!"

This time it's Waif who hugs you as you help him to his feet. You push the lever back to its original position and watch as the west side doorway resets itself. Maybe it wasn't such a good choice. Especially when you consider a new thought that just crossed your mind...

Now Waif owes *you* one! Nice going. *TURN TO PAGE 120*

"The tower is green," you say. "The star emerald on the map is green. So let's stick to the program and take the green side."

You start up the four-thousand year old staircase, with Waif following close behind you. Other than the disturbing lack of any railing, the steps are sturdy, solid, and safe. For a while, nothing happens. Then, about halfway up...

"Donovan!"

The grinding beneath your feet alerts you just before Waif's warning. The jade steps have begun tilting downward! They disappear into themselves on an angle, turning the entire staircase into a spiral slide!

You skid downward, picking up speed, your fingers grasping the tower stones for any sort of handhold. Unfortunately they're just too smooth. Finally you resign yourself and brace your legs for impact. But where the floor used to be, you notice the bottom of the stair landing has retracted into the wall!

"Ungh!"

Waif is gone, no longer beneath you. Somehow he managed to swing his body over the side of the steps, landing hard but safely on the first floor. You on the other hand, go sailing into the pit. You fall another fifteen or twenty feet, squinting your eyes shut, willing your ankles not to shatter...

Luckily you hit sand. Soft, deep sand. When you roll to a stop you're staring at bones. Thousands upon thousands of tiny little bones and teeth. Waif's torch throws light on the scene from above. That's when you notice the walls of the pit are decorated with intricate and beautiful carvings of long-fanged, deadly-looking snakes.

"The Queen's viper pit!" Waif calls down from above. "I guess that staircase was for uninvited guests only." You sit up with the crackle and crunch of petrified snake bones giving way beneath your weight. There must've been hundreds of snakes in here. Maybe thousands.

"Good thing the vipers died long before we got here," Waif says. When you look up again, a rope almost hits you square in the face. "Get up here. Let's take the other staircase."

Snakes! Why did it have to be snakes?

Climb out of the pit and *HEAD TO PAGE 147*

72

There's little time! You pull the diamond-shaped amulet from your pocket as the thunderous roar of surging water grows even louder.

A key to use in distant thunder...

You whirl around, facing the wall. But as you go to plug the silver amulet into the depression, you drop it!

Before the waters pull you under...

"DONOVAN!" Waif's scream is frantic. You ignore him. Bending through the pain in your knee, you grab the amulet once more and this time pop it into the wall...

The ground stops moving instantly. Still, there's almost no flagstone left. You stand pinned on the edge, dripping with sweat. Unable to move, until...

"Yes!"

There's another shift as the floor begins grinding back to its original position. If you hadn't been ready for it, it might have jarred you over the ledge! Waif lets out a long breath as you're slowly returned to the opposite end of the chamber. When you finally step into the hallway with him, he throws you into a bone-crushing hug.

"That was–"

The floor drops out beneath you. It happens without a hint of warning. You fall only a short distance, skid along a darkened stone ramp, and are ultimately deposited – via a hole in the ceiling – into yet another large chamber.

As you sit there rubbing your aching backside, Waif lands next to you with a loud thump.

"This is getting old," you groan as you struggle to your feet.

You're battered and bruised, but you're still here! *TURN TO PAGE 142*

The opening looks dark and cold, and let's face it, spooky. You turn your gaze back to the top of the Ziggurat.

"Stay there," you tell Waif. "I'm coming up."

With hands shaking from exertion (at least you *think* it might be exertion) you grab the next step. Everything in your upper body aches. As your footing has gotten increasingly worse, you've been transferring most of your body weight to your arms and chest. Now that decision is starting to take its toll.

You're almost to the top when you make the mistake of looking down. Vertigo seizes you. You've never been overly afraid of heights, but you've never been totally comfortable with them either. The dizzy spell passes as you cling to a four-thousand year old chunk of rock; the only thing keeping you from a very long, very messy fall.

"Look out!"

Suddenly the stone beneath your feet gives way. You dangle helplessly in the air by one arm, reaching out with your other hand for something... anything...

Quick, flip two coins! (Or flip the same coin twice)

If both coins come up *HEADS,* you should *TURN TO PAGE 126*

If both turn up *TAILS* instead, *FLIP ON BACK TO PAGE 62*

If the coins turn up with one *HEADS* and one *TAILS,* cross your fingers and *GO TO PAGE 12*

74

You grab the green lense. It feels heavy in your hand. Walking over to the mosaic, you very carefully mount it in front of the star sapphire. The room goes from bright blue to a deep turquoise or even sea green.

At first nothing happens. Then...

CLICK!

The noise comes from the dais itself. A stone drops away at waist-height, revealing a small square aperture.

"That must be it," Waif says. "There's something inside – a lever or counterweight that raises the stone door."

Before you can stop him your friend reaches inside the dark hole. His arm goes in up to the elbow.

"I don't feel anything. It's empt– ACK!"

As Waif yanks his arm back you expect the worst! You're pretty close. A red-yellow scorpion is attached to his hand, one pincer clamped painfully around your friend's thumb. Its tail curves menacingly overhead, poised and ready to strike...

Uh Oh! Flip a coin from your left hand and catch it in your right.

If the coin comes up *HEADS,* immediately *TURN TO PAGE 29*
If the flip comes up *TAILS* instead, *HEAD DOWN TO PAGE 138*

If you drop the coin, hang your head in shame and flip it until you *do* catch it! Even if it takes several tries, that's fine. We can wait all day.

You're caught between a wall of swarming rats or fleeing as fast as you legs will carry you into uncertain darkness. It's a bad choice either way, so you decide to trust your partner.

"Here!"

Waif's torch lands at your feet. You pick it up and hold it away from your body, rotating in a slow arc. The rats scramble away! In every direction you point the torch the rats fall back, afraid of the flames. You're about to call up for further instructions when something else lands beside you, slapping limply against the floor.

"Take the rope!"

Rope? Where'd he get rope? Not that you aren't grateful or anything...

Carefully you loop the rope around your legs and waist, creating a very rudimentary cradle. Sure enough, you feel yourself being lifted. Your feet leave the floor and the next thing you know Waif has pulled you all the way to the mouth of the jagged hole created when the street gave way.

"Thanks Waif," you say as you swing yourself up. He takes his torch back and nods.

"We should get moving, Donovan. Our time here is limited."

Continue through the streets of Atraharsis by *TURNING TO PAGE 13*

76

You don't even see the asp. Sleek and black, it strikes you before you have any chance to react.

Two red dots blossom on the back of your hand. They glisten like jewels in the sun. Waif kicks the snake across the room, but by then it's already too late. The asp's neurotoxin kicks in, and you feel your body going rigid as your muscles involuntarily contract. Your vision blurs. Your mouth feels numb.

"Donovan!" Waif cries out. He's shaking you now. "D-o-n-o-o-o-o-v-a-a-a-a-a-n..."

Waif's voice is the last thing you remember as the darkness closes in. For you, this is

THE END

The lizard looks slow, and your axe is sharp. What could possibly go wrong?

As the creature saunters in you wind back take your best swing. *THWACK!* The axe crashes into the side of the lizard's head exactly where you were aiming. But its skin is too thick, its skull too hard. Rather than penetrate the tough reptilian hide the weapon is jarred from your fingers and goes sailing through the air!

Waif is having no better luck. The monster takes little notice of his torch at all. It pushes through you both, heading straight past on its way to the smooth white stones directly behind you. It opens its mouth to strike... and misses!

You glance back. The lizard has one of the stones in its mouth. It starts turning back in the direction it came from.

"Eggs!" Waif cries in realization. "The quakes probably woke it from its nest, and now it thinks these things are its eggs!"

Whew. What a relief. You lower your axe when all of a sudden...

"AARRGHH!!"

With a sickening crunch the creature accidentally steps on your foot! It stomps away with the 'egg' in its mouth, but by then the damage is already done. Your foot feels like a jigsaw puzzle with half the pieces missing.

After avoiding the last swish of the monster's tail, Waif comes running to your aid. "We... I... Oh." One look at your foot is all it takes. "Donovan, I'm... I'm sorry."

The journey from Atraharsis will be painfully long. The walk to a hospital even longer. In time your foot will heal. Probably. Still, it doesn't change the fact that right now this happens to be

THE END

78

The Grand Courtyard is a huge mess of sand and rubble. You step through cautiously, avoiding the sharper, more jagged pieces that threaten to slice your legs to ribbons. You're in the process of deciding which direction is least dangerous when, all of a sudden, the entire city is rocked by a massive, violent tremor.

"Cover up!"

The walls of Atraharsis shake to their very foundations. Buildings topple around you. A massive dust cloud rolls through the Courtyard, barreling down at you with breakneck speed. You stand frozen by the sight of it. Unable to move...

At the last second, Waif grabs your arm. With surprising strength, he pulls you into the shelter of one of the smaller, more well-built hovels on one side of the street. Dust swirls outside as the walls continue to shake. Then, just as abruptly as it all started, everything stops.

"Aftershock?" Waif asks when it's all clear again.

"Maybe," you cough. Your eyes sting a little, but you're okay. Thanks to Waif.

"We'll have to hurry," you say needlessly. "This whole city could come crashing down around us at any time."

"Also," Waif adds, "Mr. Sullivan's crew would've heard the tremors. They could already be on their way here."

It's a fair point. Peeking back out into the streets you see an open area not far to the west. To the east, you notice the crumbling wreckage of what looks to be an elaborate palace.

If you want to check out the open area, *TURN TO PAGE 112*

If the crumbling palace sounds more interesting, *HEAD OVER TO PAGE 69*

You pull and push on a series of slides and buttons, advancing your way through the puzzle box. Its glass pieces move beautifully, even after dozens of centuries buried beneath the sands. You're pretty sure you're getting close when all of a sudden...

CLICK!

"That's it!" you cry out in triumph. "I did it..."

But then you look down. A bright red dot blossoms up from your index finger. You hold it out curiously, then you see the needle. The pinprick happened so quickly, the needle so insidiously positioned within the box you never even saw it.

"Why are you bleeding?" Waif asks. "What's... the..."

His voice is suddenly slow. Like he's talking with a mouthful of marbles. Or maybe it's just that the room is moving. The entire tower is spinning now, faster and faster until the next thing in your field of vision are the cobbles of the flagstone floor.

"Dooooonnooooovaaaaannnnnn..."

Waif must've left the room, because now he seems miles away. Or maybe, you realize with a growing horror, it's *you* that's leaving...

You were so close to the top of the tower. But you'll never see what's up there, because this is

THE END

80

You scream out a warning but it's already too late!

Waif gets only partially out of the way as the tower of stone comes down. His arms go up defensively as it crashes over him, knocking him to the cobblestone avenue and pinning him to the ground.

You're there in just seconds, kneeing beside him. He's alive. Still breathing. But right now he's unconscious, and there's an enormous gash on his forehead. You're no physician but your friend is going to need stitches – and lots of them.

"D-Donovan?"

Relief floods over you as Waif wakes up. He's groggy, woozy. His eyes have a glossed-over look to them that doesn't feel right. He probably has some sort of concussion.

"Don't worry," you assure him. "I'll get you help."

You wrap his wound and sit him up. In time, he even stands. Retracing your steps, you lead Waif slowly back through the city gates and toward the safety of your camp. But as you look forlornly back over the city of Atraharsis, you begrudgingly realize your adventure has reached

THE END

The south passage slopes definitively downward. As you descend into the darkness the air gets cooler. The walls of the passage also turn from brick and mortar to rough-hewn rock. Tool marks on both sides show where, thousands of years in the past, the first citizens of Atraharsis used this area to quarry stone for the city.

"There's humidity down here," you say. Your voice echoes much too loudly in the enclosed space.

"Perhaps because we're underground," Waif says.

"Yes, but there's way too much of it."

The corridor widens. Everything is dark and dank. You can no longer see the walls on either side of you. Beyond the meager corona of Waif's torch, everything is black.

"Maybe we should try the other passage."

You're in the process of deciding whether to continue when the corridor fills with the sudden grind of stone on stone. The two of you whip around to find the source of the noise: a series of thick rectangular blocks has fallen behind you, forming a portcullis. You're cut off.

"Well that settles that."

Waif looks the blocks up and down. The openings between them are only about a foot and a half wide. He sucks in his breath and, miraculously, just manages to squeeze his body through.

"Well at least *you're* not stuck here for all eternity," you say sheepishly. You know there's no possible way you'd ever fit. "Maybe you could, um, go for help?"

Your partner sucks in his gut once again and squeezes back to your side of the stone portcullis. "No my friend," he says loyally. "We're in this together."

You have a very important choice to make here.

You can continue on into the blackness by *TURNING TO PAGE 154*

Or you can venture on into the darkness by *TURNING TO PAGE 154*

82

Up ahead, several roads converge around what must once have been a busy well. A ring of beautiful gray stones is cut into a raised circular pattern, while four larger keystones are inscribed with symbols to represent the points of a compass rose.

The well shaft itself is smooth and featureless. It leads down into a darkness so thick, not even the morning sunlight can penetrate to the bottom.

Waif peers into the well curiously as he walks past. On a whim, you pull a quarter out of your pocket.

"What are you doing?" Waif asks nervously.

"Making a wish."

"In *there*?" Something about the whole thing obviously doesn't sit right with him.

"Sure. Why not?"

Waif doesn't have an answer. He only stands there, eyeballing the well shaft suspiciously.

Do you make a wish? If so, *TURN BACK TO PAGE 17*

If Waif has you spooked, put the quarter back in your pocket and *HEAD TO PAGE 33*

Quickly you sweep up the torch. Then, trying to hold Waif as still as possible, you use it to get the spiders off his body.

"Ooooww!!!'

The flames are hot, and the spiders go up quickly. But in the process, Waif's is also burned. His clothes are in tatters, and the skin of his arms and legs are bright red. As you pull him to the opposite end of the chamber, the spiders stop their advance.

"You okay?"

Waif doesn't answer – his face is too contorted in pain. He'll be alright eventually, but right now he needs some definite medical attention.

"I have some antibiotics back in my tent," you tell him. "And salve."

Your friend nods. Those two things sound great to him right about now. Continuing on right now isn't possible, but you're comforted by the fact that you still have one of the star jewels!

If you escape Atraharsis, get back to camp, and make it out of the desert? You'll be able to save your grand-uncle's estate!

You never did find the Hall of Kings, but that's okay. You and Waif had an amazing adventure, even if this happens to be

THE END

84

There's something about the statue that doesn't seem right. Something... missing.

"Look around," you tell Waif, as you begin your own search. There's sand everywhere. It's easy to move aside, but the only thing you find beneath it is rubble. That, and more sand.

"Nothing," Waif says after a while. "Unless you count this." He's holding a small chunk of rock. It looks like every other lump of stone you've seen so far. Then he hands it over, and you realize it's actually a tiny statue of a bird.

You run your thumb over the smooth marble surface of the little sparrow. Without thinking, you reach out and place it into the statue's outstretched palm.

The woman's arm moves.

In one slow, smooth motion, the arm of the statue dips down a few inches and stops. As it does, the woman's jaw drops open. Inside her mouth is a large amethyst.

"Whoa!" Waif cries. "How'd you know that?"

You take the gemstone and hold it up to the sun. It gleams a deep, beautiful purple.

"I didn't."

"But... you..."

All you can do is shrug. "It was a lucky guess."

Well it's not one of the star jewels, but it's a pretty good start!
NOW TURN TO PAGE 102

The avenue stretches north and east, to where the sheer bedrock cliff meets the city wall. Here, along the sand-strewn rock face, several openings have been carved out by hand. And high overhead, somewhere above, the obelisk.

"The city was originally built against these cliffs," Waif tells you. "The first settlers cut out these caves here."

Some of the openings are deep and wide. Using the torch you explore a few of them. Eventually you see signs of human habitation. Waif picks up one piece of a broken clay urn, turning it over and over in an attempt to read any writing he might find. You're just about to leave when you look down and stop dead in your tracks.

Resting before you is a fairly modern-looking journeyman's pack. It's emblazoned with an insignia that matches the one on your journal.

"It's *his!*" you exclaim. You scoop it up too quickly, knocking a century's worth of dust up your nose. "This pack belonged to Murdoch!"

You sneeze. Twice. Three times, then four. When you're finally done, you can't understand why Waif seems frozen in some weird, awkwardly-crouched position. That is, at least, until you follow his gaze...

A large desert cat stands poised between you and the cave exit. As you meet the stare of the cheetah's yellow eyes, its lips curl back in a snarl.

Your choices here are unfortunately limited. What do you do?

To try fighting the animal off with Waif's torch, *TURN TO PAGE 42*

To try throwing some water at it (hey, cats hate water, right?) *HEAD BACK TO PAGE 15*

If you'd rather chance it by running deeper into the cave, take that risk *ON PAGE 95*

86

You approach the small but beautiful mausoleum. But when you look back from the doorway, you notice Waif hasn't budged.

"If you go in there," he tells you, "it will have to be alone. I am sorry."

You shrug at him and peek inside. Enough sunlight bleeds in to make out the details. The small chamber is smooth and well-kept, its walls painted with faded scenes of long ago. In some, you can make out the city as it once was; wide, elegant avenues filled with throngs of colorful people. You see the ziggurat looming over a series of lush, water-filled gardens. The Queen's Tower, climbing delicately into a stunning orange sky.

But one feature stands out. Chiseled crudely into the stone, in a graffiti-like way, is a series of hurried hieroglyphs. You pull out your grand-uncle's journal and translate the ancient writing:

Beware of False Kings

You lean back for a minute, lost in thought. False kings? What does it mean? Then, all of a sudden...

CRASH!

The wall you happen to be leaning on gives way! One entire side of the mausoleum caves outward, spilling you into the street. Jagged stones and mortar shower down all around you as you're enveloped in a cloud of dirt and debris. You emerge unscathed but covered in a sheen of fine grey dust. It gets in your mouth and lungs, causing you to cough violently.

Waif is soon standing over you, extending one hand. He helps you up and dusts you off.

"Superstitious yet?" he smirks.

You're a little shaken, but it's all good. The path forks here:

Take the road to the right by *TURNING TO PAGE 97*

Or continue along the wider avenue by *GOING TO PAGE 43*

"Quick!" you tell Waif. "Into one of the buildings!"

Ducking back around the corner you choose the nearest doorway. You're through in seconds, crouching down, trying to make yourself as small a target as possible. You can smell the jackals before you even see them. Their rank, musty scent wrinkles your nose so badly you're afraid you might even sneeze.

"BACK!"

You turn just in time to see Waif kicking one of the mutts in the face. Of course they sniffed you out... like all dogs, they have an exceptional sense of smell. You should've known!

The jackal yelps in pain and skitters away to regroup with the others. During the lull you pull Waif to his feet and drag him back outside. Maybe there's still time to run. Better get moving.

Run fast. Run very fast. *TURN TO PAGE 57*

88

"Back away," you tell Waif. "We can't fight them all, there are too many!"

Carefully you retreat, but with every step you take the ants advance that much further forward. Tons more spill forth from the fissure in the ground. Soon they're crawling over one another just to get to you.

"Run!"

The ants move in a wave. You stay ahead of them, but only barely. Waif, of course, is ahead of you. Nimbly he steps through Atraharsis's rubble-strewn avenues, leaping and springing over obstacles until suddenly...

Waif trips. He falls hard, knocking the wind out of himself. You're running so fast you actually pass by him, and by the time you turn around the lower half of his body is already swarming with insects.

"No!"

You pull off your rucksack. Using it as a club, you beat most of the ants from Waif's body. There are fewer of them now. You've traveled a good distance from their hive, and rather than pursue you many have turned around. You beat the ants until your arm hurts, until finally you've driven away the last of the intruding insects. But Waif still hasn't recovered. He's covered in bites from the waist down; dozens of angry red bumps that look agonizingly painful.

Waif writhes around on the ground for what seems like forever. Eventually you help him to his feet, but his wounds are swelling up fast. His skin feels hot. He needs medical attention.

Fortunately you're still close to the city gates. If you leave now getting Waif help should be easy. Unfortunately however, this means your adventure in Atraharsis has reached

THE END

"Hang on a second," you tell Waif. "Put your ear against that wall." Lowering his knife, Waif does as you tell him. His eyes go wide.

"The underground river," you say. "The one that fed the city? It's still here. And it's just on other side of that wall." You point out a series of wide, deep fissures, all of which are seeping water. "That very *cracked* wall."

Waif gulps as he puts his knife away. Together you back out of the room, making your way into the next rough-hewn chamber. The rush of water is even louder here. But at least the walls are dry.

A minute later your partner is holding his torch against one side of the room. "Donovan," he says. "Come look at this."

Set into the chiseled rock wall, a series of crude levers and switches are set up. Most are rotted completely away, but a few of the wooden artifacts still carry some weight to them. By holding the torch close, you can see each lever is painted with a differently-colored band.

"This is unbelievable," Waif breathes. "I mean, I knew the builders were engineers, but..."

"But you didn't know they'd harness the power of the river to run their machines?" you finish for him. "This must be how the obelisk works. Waif, this must be how they buried the city!"

You put your own ear to the wall now. The river runs directly behind the ancient control panel. You can hear it churning, swirling, millions of pounds of pressure kept at bay by nothing more than a thin layer of sandstone.

"These switches could be what we're looking for," Waif suggests. "They could open a door or chamber. Maybe even the Hall of Kings."

"Or they could kill us both," you answer back. "How could they possibly still work? Another tremor, even a small one, is likely to flood this entire place."

You glance down at the controls. They're connected in sets, with only two pairs of levers still intact. Off to your left, a shadow-filled corridor exits the machine room at the opposite end.

You can pull the black and blue levers in series. If you do that, *HEAD TO PAGE 121*

Or you can push the gold and red levers together. If that's your choice, *FLIP BACK TO PAGE 28*

Or maybe you should leave well enough alone. Skip the levers entirely by *GOING TO PAGE 44*

90

Fluttering in the wind, the threadbare remnants of a four-thousand year old tent have somehow survived beneath the sands. All other supports have long since turned to dust, but one exceptionally thick pole juts defiantly upward.

Suddenly there's a great shifting and grating noise. It sounds similar to when the Obelisk key was turned, only now it's ten times louder and coming from every direction. Soon everything begins to shake. Rubble falls from the Atraharsis's high walls, sending up plumes of dust all around the city. For a heart-stopping moment you think the entire place is going to come crashing down around you, and then the rumbling stops and the air goes still. Luckily you were near the center of the road. Nothing dangerous came your way.

"You okay?" you ask Waif.

"Yes. But the city appears to not be entirely stable."

You can only smirk as you bite back a sarcastic remark. It's all you can do not to roll your eyes.

"These tremors will be felt for miles," Waif notes. "My old team will have heard them, along with Mr. Sullivan. They will come here, and soon too."

That's something you hadn't though of. It wipes the smile from your face as you factor in this new variable.

"Should we search this place?" Waif asks. "Or continue on?"

If you'd like to poke around the area some more, you can search it more thoroughly *OVER ON PAGE 139*

On the other hand, maybe you should keep moving. If you'd rather just go, *HEAD BACK TO PAGE 85*

"Alright," you say. "If this place really spooks you, there's another street that looks like it runs parallel."

Waif is quick to jump at the opportunity. He nods in gratitude and leads you from the arched area. Soon you're walking another avenue, although this one is more winding and cluttered with debris. The cracks in the street are wider here, and some of them run deep into the ground.

"I don't know," you say. "Maybe we should go back."

Your partner chuckles. "Nonsense." You notice he's having a much less difficult time than you. Smaller and lighter, Waif is also a lot quicker on his feet. He picks his way past the rubble like it's nothing.

Eventually the road narrows to the point where you almost have to walk single file. A large crack – no, a fissure – runs through the middle of the alleyway. Up ahead everything broadens out, but right now you're faced with having to jump the gap. How wide is it? Ten feet? Twelve? It's difficult to tell.

"Hey, I don't think–"

Waif jumps before you can finish. He leaps across the gap handily, with tons of room to spare.

"C'mon! It's easy!"

Well it certainly *looks* easy. Sort of. Then again...

Courage check! Flip two coins (or just flip the same coin twice)

If both coins come up *HEADS*, see if you make it by *TURNING TO PAGE 127*

If both coins come up *TAILS*, let's hope you're okay *OVER ON PAGE 39*

If you get one HEADS and one TAILS, cross your fingers and *FLIP TO PAGE 104*

92

You place the star sapphire on the dais. Off to your right, a door slides slowly open.

"Watch out!"

Waif tackles you to the floor as a trio of thick stone columns slam down from the ceiling. The pillars land barely a foot apart, too thin for you to squeeze or reach through. You're cut off from the star gem!

You glance right. The door is fully open now. Immediately however, it begins sliding closed again. With only seconds left you start toward it, willing your feet to move.

"Waif, come on!"

You can see your partner is torn. His gaze keeps moving between the rapidly closing door and the crude stone portcullis. In the shadows of the alcove, the sapphire still gleams a brilliant blue.

"Hurry!"

Eventually there's no choice – you turn sideways and hurl yourself into the shadowy hallway. When you look back you expect to see Waif right behind you... but he's not there. The door is almost closed now. Only a thin sliver of light separates you from total darkness.

"Waif!"

At the last possible second your partner comes flying into the corridor. His torch flickers as the door slams closed. When he's finally finished gathering himself, he looks up at you sheepishly.

"Well, that was..."

Your voice trails off and a moment of silence passes between you. Rather than admonish him further you take Waif's torch and walk to the end of the new hallway. "Come on," you say with forced cheerfulness. "Let's see what was worth sacrificing a star jewel for."

You enter a low, box-shaped room littered with sand. The walls here are worn smooth, except for strange vertical grooves from floor to ceiling. A simple stone altar stands in the center of the chamber. It has a opening in the top, and several smaller holes cut symmetrically into all four sides. The base of the altar is covered in glyphs.

You give the torch back to Waif. "What's it say?"

Two ancient braziers sit on either side of the altar. Waif touches the torch to them on a whim, and they immediately light up! The room fills with sweet-smelling smoke as the centuries-old charcoal burns. Waif translates easily by the new light:

Death by Fire
Water, Life
Yet Earth is Key
To End Your Strife

Almost on cue, a noise fills the chamber. The ceiling feels suddenly lower... or rather, the floor beneath you is grinding upward!

"We're going to be squashed!" Waif cries. The floor is already past the entrance, eliminating any possibility of retreat. "What do we do?"

You scramble, searching for an answer. The ceiling is flat and unremarkable, except for a slight recess directly above the altar. No help there...

Do you put out the flaming braziers, hoping the floor will stop? If so *HEAD TO PAGE 46*

The altar has an opening, maybe you could pour water into it? Try that *BACK ON PAGE 60*

You could also try scooping sand into the altar. If that's your answer *GO TO PAGE 151*

94

Your hand closes over one of the jade bookends. Then, with pantherish speed, Waif knocks your arm away.

"What the–"

An asp slithers out from beneath the ruined chest. It looks long and black and very deadly. The snake's head strikes the air where, only a split second before, your hand had rested. After missing its target it slides quickly away, disappearing beneath some rubble.

"Waif!" you cry out in astonished gratitude. "Nice going!" You hug him, and probably a little too tightly. He grunts.

"You saved my life!"

Your friend looks back at you sheepishly. "Perhaps. It was nothing, really. Where I come from–"

"Wherever you come from, you move faster than that asp! And for that I'm grateful." You toss him the bookends before slapping him roughly on the back. "These are yours, my friend. Now let's get going."

Whew, close call!

Head back into the streets of Atraharsis by *TURNING TO PAGE 124*

In the rear of the cave, a dark opening leads into the next chamber. Or it leads absolutely nowhere. Truth is, you really don't know.

"Back up," you tell Waif. You do your best to keep your voice calm, controlled. "Slowly."

Your friend takes a careful step backward. So do you. The cheetah mirrors your movements, although you do gain some measure of distance between yourselves and the big cat. Finally, with your back pressed up against the darkness, you dare a quick look over your shoulder. In the meager light of Waif's torch, you see nothing but a dead end!

"Can't go that way," you say in measured tones. Murdoch's journeyman's pack dangles from your hand. "When I throw this thing, RUN."

Half a moment later, your chance comes. The cat looks down, but only for a split second...

"GO!"

You hurl the pack as hard as you can, then sprint along the rightmost edge of the cave. Waif goes left. You don't even look back, all you can hear is the sound of the heavy bag striking the cheetah square in the face. Then you're out in the sunlight, bolting away from the cave opening. Waif is pumping hard right beside you.

Eventually you stop and turn around. You're not being pursued. Relief washes over you, followed immediately by regret. Why couldn't you have thrown something *else*?

"I really wanted to know what was in that thing," you lament.

Waif shakes his head. "I know." He points back to where the huge cat paces back and forth along the cave opening. "But it belongs her now."

Hey, at least you're not breakfast! Keep moving by *TURNING TO PAGE 97*

96

"Knowledge!" you cry. "That's the answer!"

You're practically shaking your partner by now. He stares back at you quizzically.

"Waif, if there's anything we learned about Atraharsis, it's that its founders and rulers valued knowledge above *everything* else!"

"But... but that's not tangible," Waif says. He glances down at the pedestal. "How do you place *knowledge*?"

Your mind goes blank for a moment. Then, slowly, you draw your grand-uncle's journal from your rucksack. Gingerly you place it on the simple stone pedestal.

The pedestal lowers. You watch as Robert Murdoch's hundred year-old journal sinks slowly into the floor, disappearing to a place it poetically belongs. There's the low grating of stone on stone, and a door opens in the wall before you.

You see scrolls. Scroll tubes of bone. A few dozen at least, they lay stacked in a neat pile, sealed at the ends with beeswax.

"Their knowledge," Waif breathes.

You nod solemnly. "Yes. Their discoveries and advancements. Their art, their culture." You pick up one of the scroll cases, trying to imagine the last time another person actually touched it. "They preserved it all here, for others to find. Even across four millennia."

Wordlessly Waif begins gathering up scrolls. You do the same. It means dumping half the treasure in your rucksack, but you do it anyway. You already have enough gold and jewels to last you a lifetime. But the true treasure, you realize, is the collective wisdom of Atraharsis.

As you slide the last tube into your pack a low rumble fills the Hall. Somewhere deep below, a series of hollow booms seems to be getting louder and louder. It's followed by an even more ominous background noise that rises above the rest; the thundering rush of water.

"The underground river!" Waif exclaims. "We have to hurry!"

You can help hurry things up by *TURNING TO PAGE 162*

The road here widens around a central pool, built with some of the most beautiful masonry work you've ever seen. Each stone fits perfectly within the next, the edges so sharp and crisp it looks almost as if done with laser efficiency. It's a testament to the builders that the structure has lasted this long, especially after being shaken to the surface from deep beneath the desert.

"The architects here were masters," Waif says. "It's a shame so much of their knowledge was lost with the city itself."

You're still not sure what happened to the city. Was Atraharsis razed? Sacked? Or did its engineers somehow find a way to bury it, to hide its secrets from the rest of the world?

You hop up into the pool itself, which is filled with a fine sand. A preliminary search reveals a colorful mosaic on the bottom, made up of thousands of tiles. You motion Waif over. "Help me with this."

Together you work to uncover the picturesque artwork that graces the bottom of the once-beautiful pool. When you've scattered most of the sand to the far corners, the image of a woman is revealed. She's garbed in a starkly-colored dress of alternating red and black, and menaced by a snarling dog. The woman is running in the opposite direction.

"Nothing else in here," Waif sighs. He swipes an arm across his forehead and it comes back slick and glistening. "Should we keep moving?"

Keep moving. *HEAD ON DOWN TO PAGE 145*

98

"Might as well check out everything," you tell Waif. "Just... be careful."

Waif steps forward and prods the sacks with his foot... which turns out to be the worst possible choice. The pile crumbles to dust at his touch, and hundreds of spiders begin pouring forth.

"Aaaaaa!!!!" he screams. It's hard to see anything with Waif swinging the torch back and forth. "Get them off of me!"

You rush forward to help him beat the spiders from his leg. But they're on his arms now, too. Waif strikes at them with the torch, singing all the hair from his forearms and burning himself in the process. The spiders themselves go up in waves of flame, like tiny pieces of dried paper.

"Stop moving! Stop struggling!" you tell him. But he can't. Waif falls backward into the pile where even *more* of the arachnids swarm over him. He drops the torch...

You need to do something quick!

Do you use the torch to get the rest of the spiders off your friend? If so, *TURN TO PAGE 83*

Or do you grab the torch and use it on the spiders' nest? If that's your move *GO TO PAGE 130*

You look up at the crown. It's the only symbol that's not an animal. It's also the only symbol that's regal.

The Hall of Kings...

"It's gotta be the crown," you tell Waif. "Come on, let's go!"

Waif follows dutifully. The only hint of skepticism on his part is a small backward glance as you make your way through the shadowy exit.

Almost immediately things change. The floor is polished. The walls take on a more finished feel. Everything seems nicer, more beautifully designed. Then the hall opens into another chamber, this time a throne room!

"This is it!" you cry. "The Hall of Kings!"

You stop, the smile fading from your face. Something is wrong. There's something soft, almost spongy beneath your feet. Waif swings his torch low, and that's when you realize you're standing in a mushroom patch.

"What the–"

Your feet are stuck. These aren't like any mushrooms you've ever seen. The strange grey fungus is everywhere, all dry and powdery. It covers the walls, the floor, the ancient throne itself. You're able to pull your feet free, but every movement sends up clouds of powder. It gets in your eyes, your nose, your mouth...

"Spores..." Waif chokes. "Stop moving. They're... the spores..."

All of a sudden you're very, very tired. Your legs weigh a thousand pounds each. Your arms hang like tree trunks at your sides. You open your mouth to say something but all you can manage is a bone-cracking yawn. You look over at Waif and he's already laid down, right in the middle of the mushrooms.

"Waif..." Your voice is slurred and far away. "We... cant... we have to..."

Now your eyelids are heavy too. They droop closed, and a wonderful sense of peace steals over you. Maybe you just need to sit down and rest a minute. Or maybe, just maybe, this is

THE END

100

"I don't know which blocks go where," you say forlornly. "And I'm afraid of trying the wrong ones. Knowing the engineers that built this city, who knows what would happen?"

Waif has no choice but to agree. Together you turn to face the marble column.

You really think you can climb that thing?"

"Guess we'll find out," Waif says.

He starts up it, and at first things seem okay. Waif's fingers find cracks you can't even see with your own eyes. His feet find tiny toeholds. Slowly but surely, he makes his way upward. But then, for seemingly no reason, he stops.

"Hang on..." Waif says. His voice seems shaky.

"What is it?"

"Is the column moving?"

You look down. Sure enough, the entire column is rotating. Waif is being pulled away from you, clockwise, with the grinding of stone on stone. Abruptly the cylinder lurches downward. Sinks another ten or fifteen feet.

"Jump!" you tell him. "Get down! Now!"

BOOM!

Something deep inside the tower shifts. Or maybe it collapses. There's a hollow, rumbling sound followed by what sounds like it could be rushing water. And then...

Everything falls away. Waif, the column, the emerald – the whole world is a mass of whirling, falling stone as the entire Queen's Tower comes apart from the bottom up. You don't cry out. You don't even have time. All you have is one last perfect view of Atraharsis as you cartwheel downward through the morning sky.

For you, as well as for Waif, this is regrettably

THE END

You don't know who this person is, but assaulting them from behind just doesn't seem right.

"Hey!" you call out. "You!"

The figure doesn't react. He doesn't move. You wait another few seconds, then step out into the street from behind the safety of the broken column.

"How did you get–"

The sentence falls back down your throat. Waif, for some reason, is suddenly laughing. "Look!" he points.

Off to the side, the statue of a man stands on a sand-strewn pedestal. He's holding a staff in one hand and a set of scrolls in the other. It's then you realize the figure leaning against the pillar isn't a man at all. It's nothing more than a shadow, made tall by the morning sun.

"Should we get him?" Waif jeers. "Or should we let him go?"

There's nothing you can do but chuckle yourself. The laughter actually feels good. It breaks the tension. Warmth begins spreading over you as the sun climbs into the sky.

A brief search of the fire pit turns up nothing but rubble, refuse, and a few petrified, gnawed-upon bones.

"We should get going," Waif says. "The day is escaping us."

Two wide, identical avenues stretch away from the fire pit in new directions.
If you take the road to the east, *JUMP TO PAGE 103*
If you take the road to the west, *GO TO PAGE 124*

102

You continue beyond the Oasis into another even larger area. Here your surroundings become less streets and avenues and more of a mass of toppled structures, all of them in varying stages of decay. The wind howls through the broken stone of hollowed out homes. As it rises and falls, it creates a creepy wailing sound.

"This looks like the Ruins," you say, "from Murdoch's map."

Many of the buildings around you are massive, or at least *were* massive when they were first constructed. It's obvious they were once very beautiful. Worn cobbles beneath your feet poke through in many places here. Thinking about the people who walked on it – more than four and a half thousand years ago – leaves you with a sense of awe.

"Donovan! Wait!"

Waif's warning comes too late as you round the next corner. A pack of what appear to be wild dogs is patrolling the street. One raises its nose and sniffs the air. It sees you, and they all come running.

"Waif! The dogs–"

"Not dogs, jackals," Waif says. He's holding his torch out before him in a defensive posture. "They'll be on us in seconds! What should we do?"

There still might be time to run. If you want to find out, *HEAD TO PAGE 57*

You could also try to make a stand. If that's your choice, *GO TO PAGE 11*

Or maybe you could hide in one of the buildings. If you'd like to try, *TURN TO PAGE 87*

The avenue you travel is long and wide and filled with sand. Some piles are even taller than you are, and as you make your way among them you notice yourself walking on a definite tilt. It's almost as if the road beneath your feet slopes downward. With all the sand it's impossible to tell.

All of a sudden Waif stops and points with an outstretched arm. "There is the temple on your map."

He's right. The dome is cracked and most of the arched entrances have long since fallen over, but the resemblance is unmistakable: you're standing before the Temple of Luus'. And within its walls, if Murdoch's map is right... one of the fabled star jewels.

"Who is Luus'?" Waif asks.

"I was hoping you'd know."

Your friend shrugs and shakes his head. "The people of Atraharsis had many gods. Many temples. They worshiped a variety of–"

Waif stops because you've already left him in the street. Passing beneath one of the unbroken archways, you make your way into the temple's once-sacred inner halls. There's a lot less sand inside. The floors are smooth, and painted murals decorate the walls. Although faded with age, you can make out a few scenes depicting the people who once lived here. Most of the settings are outdoors. The people kneel prostrate before the temple, all heads turned to the sky.

"Sun worshipers?" you ask.

"Could be," Waif says. "Could be anything else, too."

The halls get more decorated and beautiful as you continue through them. Then, as you get nearer the temple's inner chambers, a room up ahead seems bathed in a glowing blue light.

"The star sapphire!" you exclaim. "Come on!"

Did you really find it? Find out by *TURNING TO PAGE 129*

104

You wind back, take a running start, and then at the last minute, jump...

Waif is there to catch you on the other side, absorbing your momentum. You spin around and look back. Not only did you cross the gap, you made it easily.

"See?" Waif says. "Told you."

You can't help but smile. It's good to have a partner you can trust. Even better, you're pretty sure Waif feels the same way.

Nice job. When you're done patting yourself on the back, *TURN TO PAGE 21*

A dozen large avenues feed into what was unmistakably some kind of central bazaar. This was obviously a place of great trade. Everywhere you look you see ancient stones set among petrified timbers – all that remains of the colorful booths that once made up a huge inner city of tents and stalls.

"We've passed a lot of statues," you say. "But none of warriors or generals. I've seen no swords, no spears..."

"That's because Atraharsis was a city of enlightenment and wisdom," Waif says. "The people here valued knowledge above everything else, even gold and gems."

You wrinkle your nose in distaste. "Let's hope not. Or I came all this way for nothing."

Searching the area thoroughly would take months, even years, so all you can do is a cursory job. Together you find little that isn't buried beneath tons of sand and rubble. You pick up an ancient bowl, intact and valuable. Also amongst your treasures you count a polished onyx statue of a woman petting a cat. When you look over at Waif however, he's bent over a jug he recently unsealed. Your friend is eagerly scooping fistfuls of pink and white rock salt into his pack.

You can't help but laugh. "Waif, why?"

"You can always use salt!" he tells you simply.

"Yeah, but salt that's thousands of years old?" You still don't get it. "After all this time, wouldn't–"

Without warning the ground breaks open before you. Only this isn't an earthquake, or a tremor. This is something entirely different.

"Ants!"

Dozens of angry-looking insects begin spilling from the torn ground. They're the biggest ants you've ever seen.

"Red desert ants!" Waif shouts. "All these tremors must have disturbed their colony!"

The ants advance toward you, their antennae quivering in the air. You can see their mandibles opening and closing. They look sharp and incredibly painful.

Through sheer bad luck your back happens to be up against one of the larger structures in Atraharsis's central bazaar. There might be time to flee, or you can choose to fight the ants off using the flames of Waif's torch.

The ants number in the hundreds now, and they're still pouring from the ground. Whatever you choose, you'd better do it fast!

If you think you can stand your ground, try fighting the ants off by *TURNING TO PAGE 140*

If you'd rather take your chances and run, you'll need to roll two dice (or just pick a random number from 2 to 12)

If the total of your roll is a 3, 5, 7, or 9 *SEE IF YOU MAKE IT ON PAGE 88*

If you roll anything other than those numbers, *CHECK OUT WHAT HAPPENS ON PAGE 150*

108

"Waif!" You move to push your friend out of the way, but not before the spider sinks its fangs into his neck.

Waif screams. You reach for his torch, but he's flailing too hard. Eventually he drops it, the torch instantly going out in a large pile of sand. As Waif falls, clutching his neck, the spider turns to face you.

You reach back into your rucksack and your fingers close over your camping hatchet. Unfortunately, this time it's stuck. As hard as you pull, it just won't come free. In the meantime, Waif is moaning as his body fights whatever toxin the spider just injected into him. You glance back and the creature is almost on you.

At the last second you kick it. The crunch of its body is oddly satisfying, even through the fear. But joy turns to terror as you watch the spider's underbelly break ripely open. Hundreds of smaller spiders come pouring from their mother's body, swarming in your direction. And they're not happy.

What's worse than a venomous spider bite? A hundred spider bites.

Sorry to say it, but this is

THE END

"Well we're already here," you tell Waif. "Might as well make our way straight inside."

You advance forward and find yourself feeling very small. Nothing remains of the great gates to the city. The walls are broken, shattered piles of stone that yawn inward where mounds of sand and rubble make up all new avenues of Atraharsis. Off in the distance, strange cracking sounds come from an unknown origin. It could be the wind. It could be your imagination. The entire thing is very, very eerie.

Waif pulls a long torch from his own pack and lights it. The flames feel good as they drive some of the morning chill from the air.

"Where does your grandfather's journal say to go next?" Waif asks.

"Grand-*uncle*," you correct him. "Besides, it wasn't originally his journal. It belonged to a man named Murdoch. He was here over a hundred years ago."

The map is nondescript here, and this portion of the journal doesn't offer much guidance.

"There's the main courtyard," you say. "Let's start there."

Head over the Courtyard by *FLIPPING BACK TO PAGE 78*

110

The rats are swarming, they'll be on you in seconds. There's no way you're staying put! You whirl around and run full tilt down the pitch black hallway. Anything's better than being gnawed on by a hundred rats. In the tunnel at least, you'll have some protection. Maybe. You hope...

WHAM!

You wake staring up into a blinding white light. *Is this the afterlife?* You're not entire sure. For several moments you can't remember anything beyond your own name. And then...

Oh yeah! The rats!

You bolt upright, feverishly slapping at every part of your body. You're relieved to find no rats in sight. Gradually your eyesight returns and a man fades into your vision. It's Waif!

"I *told* you not to move," he admonishes you.

"What happened?"

"You ran full speed into a wall. Or at least I *think* it was a wall. It was too hard to tell down there. Too dark."

Your hand goes to your head. There's a nasty, painful bump, but when you pull your palm away it comes back clean. No blood. That's good, at least.

"But... How'd you get me out?"

"The rats wouldn't come near my torch," Waif explains. "Plus, I have this." He pats a thick coil of rope. "Next time listen to me. Are you okay to walk?"

You nod and Waif helps you up. After drinking half your canteen you promptly upend some of it over your head. Waif frowns at the waste of good water, but by all accounts it was a necessary thing. You feel seventy-five percent better. Maybe eighty.

Better get moving. The star jewels aren't going to find themselves, right?

HEAD BACK TO PAGE 13

At long last you stand before the Queen's Tower. It's been impressive all morning from a distance, but up close the structure takes on all new levels of beauty and wonder.

Smooth white stone of an unknown origin winds its way high into the desert sky. The tower itself looks almost like the queen on a chessboard. Its curved hourglass shape flares out near the top, forming what resembles a green-jeweled crown.

"There's no door."

Waif is right. You pass through a marbled arch straight into the lower level of the tower itself. Everything inside, though ruined, still retains a certain measure of refined elegance. Sand partially covers the lavish, tattered carpets. Shredded tapestries rot on the walls, parts of them still sporting vivid color.

"Which Queen was this built for?" you ask.

"I don't know know," Waif says. "But she had great taste."

The second floor is several stories overhead. Two staircases wind their way upward in opposite directions to the next level. One of them is stone. The other is green, set with pieces of jade inlay.

"Which one?"

Waif shrugs. "I suppose it doesn't matter. It appears they both lead to the same place."

Do you take the stone staircase? If so *FLIP TO PAGE 147*
Or does the green jade staircase sound better to you? *HEAD TO PAGE 71*

112

"Let's head over to that open area," you tell Waif. "That way if there's another tremor, at least nothing will fall on top of us."

The avenue eventually yawns into what must've been a beautiful, scenic Oasis. Water once fed this place in abundance. Smooth tiles mark pathways through gardens now filled with nothing more than sand. There are fountains everywhere, and statues of birds and fish. Everything is done with amazing craftsmanship, from the empty pools to the mosaics set into the surface of the marble benches.

"The rulers of Atraharsis were engineers," Waif explains. "They built many wonderful things. These were their gardens, fed from beneath the city by a great aquifer."

You remember your grand-uncle telling you tales of a tunnel system beneath Atraharsis. In his stories the tunnels were filled with treasure, not water.

"I thought the Hall of Kings was beneath the city?"

Waif nods. "It was said to be, yes."

"Then maybe we should look for a way down."

While searching the area you walk past a group of exquisite female statues. They stand in a circle, laughing, splashing, playing... all except one. The lone woman faces away from the group, palm up, with one outstretched arm. It's almost like she could be pointing.

If you decide to follow in the statue's direction *GO TO PAGE 40*
If you'd rather search the Oasis for other clues *HEAD OVER TO PAGE 84*
Or maybe you'd rather just continue onward. If so, *TURN TO PAGE 102*

You step onto a red tile. You don't hesitate, or even think about it – you just do it.

Nothing happens.

"Excellent," Waif says. "Now just stick to the red ones."

Unfortunately it's not going to be that easy. The next red tile is too far away. You'll have to step on one of the other colors first. You choose again...

Waif winces as you place your right foot onto one of the black tiles. This time you move slowly, shifting your weight little by little. As your trailing foot finally leaves the red tile, you grit your teeth...

"We still okay?"

You sense Waif nodding somewhere behind you. "We're good."

By sticking just to the red and black tiles, you make you way across the hall. Your partner mimics your path, taking exactly the same steps, until the two of you stand safely on the familiar flagstones of the opposite hallway.

Waif shrugs as he looks back. "Maybe the white tiles did nothing too?"

You can only smirk. "Why don't you try them?" you suggest. "I'll wait here."

Continue braving the shadows of the Underhalls when you *TURN TO PAGE 44*

114

The interior of the Ziggurat is a collection of dust and shadows. The sun streaming in through the doorway reveals only a small slice of the chamber. The rest is lost in darkness, at least until Waif files in behind you.

As your friend's torch illuminates all the but the far corners of the rectangular room, you can make out writing on the walls. Beautiful glyphs are carved in neat, immaculate columns. For a moment you wish your grand-uncle were here. He would sit here deciphering every one of them, telling countless stories from long, long ago.

"Any idea what they say?" you ask Waif.

His eyes dart up and down as he holds his torch up to the wall. "Mostly they are a warning. The ones I know, anyway."

"Warning against what?"

Waif shrugs apologetically. He points out that some of the writings look smoother than the rest. Rather than a bunch of glyphs, this part of the wall appears to be a map.

"More tunnels," Waif says. He drags a finger along a series of dust-caked lines. "They connect the Ziggurat to the catacombs of Atraharsis."

In the back of the room you find a small exit, and beyond that, another chamber. This one however, glows with a light of its own. A red light.

"Come on!" you cry. "This way."

Not far above you, an opening in the ceiling leads to a pure crimson chamber. Hand and footholds have been carved into the wall, forming a ladder of sorts.

"That's the top, right?"

"I think so." Waif looks apprehensive about the light. Probably he's just spooked.

"Well let's go!"

Climb the ladder to the top of the Ziggurat and *TURN TO PAGE 25*

The giant piece of wall hurdles inexorably downward, screaming through the dust and chaos. There's no time to move...

BOOM!

It crashes violently into the ground only a few feet away! Smaller pieces break off, showering you with dirt and gravel. You might have a few cuts or scrapes when everything is said and done. The good news is, you're going to be okay!

As the tremors grind to a halt you feel Waif's hand close over your arm. He pulls you from the alley and leads you into the open area, eliminating any further risk of getting crushed.

"We shouldn't delay," you say when everything has returned to normal. "Between the sandstorms raging out there and the ground shifting in here who knows how long this city will stay unburied."

Waif nods his agreement. "We need to move quickly for another reason," he advises. "Sullivan and his crew would have felt the tremors. If I were him, I would be heading this way to investigate."

You stare back at your friend blankly. You hadn't thought of that. Just one more thing to worry about...

Better keep up the pace. *HEAD ON OVER TO PAGE 105*

116

You walk the streets of Atraharsis exuberantly, your head still spinning with accomplishment. The star jewel is going to solve all of your problems. You and Waif will be known, respected. Maybe even famous! But best of all, recovering the priceless gem will certainly save your grand-uncle's estate.

"Where to now?" Waif asks.

You walk over to where the street is the most broken. Beneath the rubble, the sunlight illuminates a man-made underground passage of brick and stone. "Down there," you say. "The Underhalls."

It's almost crazy. Atraharsis has proven unstable enough, yet here you are willing to go deeper. But you know you'll never achieve your final goal without traversing the series of tunnels dug beneath the city.

"Is Sullivan after the Hall of Kings as well?" you ask Waif.

"Of course."

"Then you know it's down there," you point. "We're here, and he's not. So let's go do it."

You climb down and begin walking the tunnels. Eventually all sunlight dissipates, leaving you in halls that are pitch-black and choked with dust. Waif's torch lights the way, but beyond its glow the rest of the world is totally unknown. The darkness is like a blanket, draped in every direction.

Abruptly Waif stops walking. You bump into him.

"The halls run left and right here," he says. "Which one do we take?"

If the left passage sounds good, *HEAD TO PAGE 51*
If the right hallway sounds better, *GO TO PAGE 119*

The serpent looks like the most deadly of all the glyphs. Therefore, you theorize, it must be safe.

"Let's take the snake," you tell Waif. Your friend hesitates, but only for a moment. Holding the torch before him, he follows you into the shadows.

The corridor continues for a long while. It also appears to curve to the right. At certain intervals other corridors open into the main hallway, but all of them are impassable; each one is choked closed with rubble and sand.

"Think we picked the right one?" Waif asks.

You shrug. "Impossible to tell until we get there." And just as you finish saying it, 'there' arrives in the form of another darkened chamber.

The two of you step forward and peer inside. But it's not until you've entered the room that you realize what just happened...

"It's the same room!" you cry. You see six walls, six glyphs – everything is precisely the same as you left it.

"Did we walk in a circle?" Waif asks.

You glance back at the hall you just came out of. Etched into the stone above it you see the horse.

"Yeah. Looks like the horse and serpent are connected to the same hallway." You frown. "We walked all that way for nothing."

Waif flashes a gold-toothed smile your way. "No, not nothing. We just eliminated two wrong choices."

He makes a good point. Now there are only four exits left for you to choose from.

If you pick the exit marked with the DOG, *TURN TO PAGE 146*

If you pick the exit marked with the CROWN, *TURN TO PAGE 99*

If you pick the exit marked with the CAT, *TURN TO PAGE 156*

If you pick the exit marked with the HAWK, *TURN TO PAGE 160*

118

The sound of barking and braying eventually fades into the distance. The jackals are gone! You guide Waif through a few twists and turns just to be on the safe side, and emerge back onto one of Atraharsis's wide, sand-swept avenues. Everything around you is the same sun-bleached beige.

A long, low structure captures your attention, mainly because of a large inscription over the doorway. Pulling out your grand-uncle's journal, it takes only moments to translate:

The Greatest Treasures Lie Within

"This is it!" you exclaim. You can't jam the book back into your rucksack fast enough. "Waif, come on!"

Inside, the building is half-filled with sand. An entire wall is caved in, and sunlight streams in from above. The rest of the structure is filled with shelves. Wall to wall, they're packed with thousands of scrolls and scroll cases of yellowed bone.

"Where are the treasures?" you ask. Absently you pick up a stack of papyrus pages bound crudely together with glue. The precursor of an actual book.

"I believe you're holding them."

"This?" you cry indignantly. "These books and scrolls?"

"No," Waif explains. "The *knowledge* within these books and scrolls. To the founders of Atraharsis, that was more valuable than anything else. Even gold or jewels."

You frown as the fragile paper turns to dust between your fingers. "Well then they won't mind if I look around for some *real* treasure."

You can search the library some more by *TURNING TO PAGE 30*

If you're pretty sure the treasures you're looking for lie elsewhere, *HEAD OVER TO PAGE 124*

The hall widens here into a large, rectangular room. It might have once been a sub-basement or an antechamber, but now it appears empty. You notice it's a lot cooler down here. Other than some dark stains across floor, the only other feature is an identical exit in the opposite wall.

"There's something lying over there," Waif says. "In the corner."

He moves that way before you can say anything. After having led the way through the city, it's weird having to follow your partner now. But he's the one with the torch.

"Slow down," you tell him. Your voice is nasal. It seems that with every movement you make, the dust of centuries swirls its way up your nostrils.

The object comes into view. Three moldy, decrepit sacks are stacked in a rough pile. Who knows how long they've been there. Your nose wants nothing to do with them.

"Should we check them out?" Waif asks.

Four thousand year-old sacks? Why not? Check them out when you *GO TO PAGE 98*

On second thought, why bother? Maybe you should continue on by *TURNING TO PAGE 152*

120

"The sun rises in the east," you reason, "so most of the sunlight is streaming in from that direction."

A moment later you're standing by the east lever. Waif stands at the ready, wincing with anticipation as you pull it.

For a few seconds nothing happens. You're afraid that maybe the mechanism is too old... that centuries of being buried have destroyed whatever it once did. But then you remember, this is Atraharsis. Its craftsmen were celebrated and renowned for their amazing works of engineering.

There's a distant boom, followed by the low, hollow grinding of stone on stone. As the tremendous granite block begins lowering itself, a stone door rises out of the floor in the east hallway. It continues upward, blocking the sunlight as it moves to meet the ceiling. Once there, it stops.

Sunlight still enters from the west, but that light is subdued, diffused. Your eyes adjust to a room that is now mostly dark. Through the star jewel, crimson light streams in from above. But now you see something else... a pattern of small depressions cleverly cut into the wall and ceiling. A path that leads straight up – and over – to the star ruby.

"I got this," Waif tells you. He climbs the wall nimbly, using the shallow depressions as hand and footholds. When he reaches the ceiling he grabs two similar depressions and kicks gently away from the wall. He's dangling thirty feet in the air now, by only his fingertips.

"Be careful!"

As if he's been doing it his whole life, Waif moves hand over hand across the ceiling. You marvel at his agility. When he reaches the star jewel he plucks it free, tucks it into his shirt, and reverses direction. You breathe a deep sigh of relief as he makes the wall again and scrambles back down. When he hands you the gemstone he's wearing a broad smile.

You did it! You recovered the star ruby of Atraharsis!

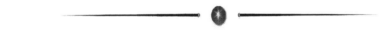

Time to head back down the Ziggurat and into the city. *TURN TO PAGE 135*

"Here," you tell Waif. "Help me with these. Ready? One... two..."

Simultaneously you pull down on the black and blue levers. They move smoothly, but with the feeling of a heavy weight somewhere behind them. There's a loud *CLICK* deep within the wall, followed by a few long seconds of nothingness. Then...

WHOOSH!

A puff of wind swirls up from behind the panel, blowing all the hair away from your face. The rushing of water gets louder. And louder...

"Switch it back!" Waif yells. He's shoving on the levers with all his might. "Switch it back!"

Quickly you grab hold of the sticks alongside him. You heave forward, putting all of your weight behind it, when suddenly...

SNAP. Both levers break off in your hands!

Your partner looks back at you in growing horror. He opens his mouth to say something, but before he can get anything out the room dissolves in an icy explosion of water and stone...

As the unstoppable force of the underground river sweeps you under, you realize with dismal certainty this must be

---

THE END

122

The staircase finally ends. Out of breath and out of steps, you make it to the very top of the Queen's Tower.

The view from up here is amazing. The broken city of Atraharsis lies spread out beneath you, like a bunch of child's blocks tumbled over. The obelisk sits high on the cliff overlooking it all, and beyond that, the desert stretches in every direction.

A long, slender column of smooth stone rises high into the sky above you. Atop it, gleaming green in the morning sun, is the star emerald of Atraharsis.

Your stomach lurches just thinking about how high off the ground you are. And yet the emerald is even higher, impossibly out of reach.

"How are we going to get it down?"

The corner of Waif's mouth twists in thought. "I can climb it," he tells you. For once however, there's no confidence in his voice. He almost looks skeptical.

"No way. There are no handholds."

"There are *always* handholds," Waif replies.

Scattered at your feet you notice a bunch of square stone blocks. Some of them are embossed with images of what appear to be animals. As you kneel to examine them, Waif taps your shoulder and points to the base of the column. "Look at this."

Set into the column itself are three square holes. Two of them are empty. The third one is already filled with one of the animal blocks: the rodent.

"I'm starting to understand the people who built this city," you tell Waif. "And I'll bet anything this mechanism brings the column down."

"We need to put the correct blocks into the first two holes," you say. "But which ones?"

You scavenge around the top of the tower. You find only five different blocks to choose from.

If you *know* which two blocks to pick (and don't guess!), take the number of the FIRST block as the tens column and the number of the SECOND block as the ones column, and *GO TO THAT PAGE NUMBER.*

For example, if you put the crocodile block (1) in the left hole, and the lion block (5) in center hole, you would go to page 15. (HINT: It's *not* page 15)

If you don't know which two blocks to use, DON'T GUESS. Waif still might be able to climb the column. In that case, flip two coins:

If the coins come up *BOTH HEADS* you should *TURN TO PAGE 100*

If the coins come up *BOTH TAILS* you need to *TURN TO PAGE 136*

If you get one *HEADS* and one *TAILS* you should *GO TO PAGE 169*

124

Further west, the broken roads and avenues turn mostly to sand. Among these, with the sheer face of the cliff looming not far in the distance, you come across a broad series of standing stones.

"The Necropolis," Waif tells you. "It's on your map."

A chill runs through you as you make your way through the ancient cemetery. Elaborate monuments mark the lives of people who've been gone for four dozen centuries. There's an air of stillness here. An unsettling calm. As creepy as it seems, this is the one place Waif doesn't seem spooked by. As superstitious as your friend is, it appears death is the one thing that doesn't frighten him.

"Donovan! Look!"

You've been avoiding the grave markers, but not Waif. Pegged to one of the taller ones, a diamond-shaped amulet of pure silver gleams in the sun. Beneath it, a message has been scrawled in charcoal.

A Key to use in Distant Thunder

Before the Waters Pull You Under

"It's in English!" you cry. The flowing black letters are distinct and familiar. You flip open the journal to compare the handwriting. It matches perfectly. "It's from Murdoch!"

Carefully Waif removes the amulet from its peg. He flips it over, finds nothing on either side, and hands it to you.

"Why would he leave this here?" Waif asks. "And why the message?"

"Murdoch's expedition split up," you explain to him. "He had more than one group searching for the star jewels. They must've been leaving hints for each other."

"Okay, but why the rhymes?"

You think about it for a moment. "I don't know. I always figured he was just a strange guy. But maybe... maybe there was another expedition looking for Atraharsis also. Kinda like us and Sullivan."

Waif reads the charcoal message again, this time out loud. "Waters," he laughs. "Pulling you under?"

With one hand you pick up a fistful of sand. The wind carries it away as it slips through your fingers. "I don't know," you say. "Atraharsis was dried up long before Murdoch's crew got here." A frightening thought occurs to you. "Maybe they were dying of thirst."

Waif nods solemnly. "Or seeing a mirage."

As you slip the strange amulet into your pocket you see a wide road leading back to the east. Not far down, it forks to the left and right.

If you take the left fork *HEAD DOWN TO PAGE 103*

If you'd rather take the right fork, *GO TO PAGE 18*

126

"Waif! Hel–"

Your friend reaches out for you, but just a moment too late. You drop through the air a good fifteen feet, bounce off the stone beneath you, and instantly begin rolling down the face of the Ziggurat. Sharp, jagged stone claws at you from every direction. Cut and scrapes however, are the least of your concerns right now...

Acting quickly, you splay your arms and legs outward in order to slow your roll. It helps, but it also leaves you vulnerable. At one point your left leg is bent backward at a disturbing angle. There's a muffled pop that originates from somewhere behind your kneecap, and you find yourself screaming in agony.

The wind is knocked from your lungs as your back slams into one of the stone slabs. Lifting your head groggily you take stock of the situation. You've fallen about halfway down the Ziggurat, and your leg is most certainly broken.

The good news is that you'll live. Everything but your pride will eventually heal. But as Waif scrambles down to help carry you back through the gates of Atraharsis, you come to the solemn realization that this is

THE END

You back up slowly, trying to gauge the distance. Sometimes the jump looks impossible. At other angles, it looks easy.

"Just do it already," Waif calls from the other side.

Here goes nothing!

You run... and jump. Halfway across you realize your leap isn't *nearly* as good as Waif's. You're going to fall short!

The air leaves your lungs all at once as you slam chest-first into the opposite wall of the small chasm. Your hands and fingers claw at the dirt, but they're slipping fast!

Waif's face goes from one of total confidence to a complete, almost comical look of dismay. He runs over, grabs your wrists, and pulls you up just before your fingers give way. You lay there panting, sucking in air but not oxygen, for what seems like forever.

"Sorry," Waif says sheepishly. "I thought you–"

You hold up one hand until your breath comes back. "You know why they call you Waif, right?"

Your friend blinks. "Because I am small. And thin."

"And fast," you chuckle. "Come on, let's go."

Close one! Time to brush off the dirt and *HEAD TO PAGE 21*

128

"If these symbols are glyphs of 'doom', we should probably learn what they are. That way we can avoid them."

You look the tower up and down, trying to find a weak spot. One of the mid-sized boulders seems to be loose. If you brushed away enough sand, you're sure you could shift it.

"C'mon Waif, help me with this one."

The two of you get to work. You spend the next ten or fifteen minutes clearing compacted sand away from the ancient stone. It's like scraping cement, only softer, easier. Eventually you can wiggle it. A little bit at first, and then a lot.

Soon you're pushing, shoving. When your shoulder hurts, you start kicking. Nothing seems to be working. You're about to give up when all of a sudden...

"Waif, look out!"

A stone splits in half near the bottom of the pile with a resounding *CRACK!* Then the whole thing topples over. It's falling... but not in the direction you wanted it to!

Quick, flip two coins! (Or flip the same coin twice)

If they both come up *HEADS* when they land *TURN TO PAGE 80*

If either (or both) of the coins show *TAILS* after flipping *HEAD BACK TO PAGE 32*

You race into the temple's inner sanctum, with Waif right behind you. A stunningly beautiful mosaic makes up one entire wall. In the center of it, gleaming brightly, is a star sapphire the size of a baseball.

"That's it!" you cry exuberantly. "Waif, we did it!"

BOOM!

No sooner do the words leave your lips than the room explodes with a hollow bang. A giant block of granite has dropped from the ceiling of the hallway you just came from, totally and completely sealing off the exit. Waif looks utterly pale. If your partner delayed even just another second he'd be as flat as a pancake right now!

"How... how do we get out?" he wavers.

Slipping your grand uncle's journal from your rucksack you turn quickly to the temple entry. By the cerulean light you read the following passage:

When Drowning in a Sea of Blue
Only Royals May Pass Through

Waif blinks. "Well we're certainly drowning in blue. But what's royal in here?"

The room itself is fairly empty. A raised dais near the mosaic contains a collection of thick glass spheres in an array of different colors. Most of them are broken. A few are left intact. Looking back at the sunlight streaming in through the star sapphire, you notice something interesting...

"I got it!" you tell Waif. "See that brass mount in front of the sapphire? It's made to fit these lenses. The priests of the temple could swap them out. Use them to change the color of the room."

There are three lenses left unbroken. But which – if any – is the right one?

If you mount the red lense *FLIP BACK TO PAGE 26*

If you try the yellow lense instead *HEAD OVER TO PAGE 37*

If the green lense seems right to you, *TURN TO PAGE 74*

130

You sweep up the torch and make your decision: before helping Waif you need to cut off the creatures at the source. You touch the flame to the ancient sacks...

The spider's nest goes up in a giant fireball! It flares, and for a brief moment the entire chamber feels like you're getting the worst sunburn of your life. The spiders cringe, curling up into tiny balls. They fall away from Waif's body like black rain.

"What was that?" Waif blinks.

"Their nest."

Your friend is still blindly patting down his arms and legs. He must've been staring directly at the flames. As you search the room, the glint of metal catches your eye. You kick apart the burning sacks to reveal a large pile of red and black tiles. On top of them is a smaller stack – this one of silver ingots.

"Help me gather these," you say, pointing.

Finally satisfied he's gotten rid of any last stragglers, your partner helps gather up the silver bars. Each is stamped with the rough glyph of a lion. Waif finishes, wobbling as he stands. "Almost too much to carry."

"Almost," you grin.

The halls are dark and full of cobwebs. *FLIP OVER TO PAGE 152*

You follow the widest road away from the broken Tower. After walking for quite a while you come to the skeletal remains of a once-magnificent grove.

"This place was the pride of Ta and Sa-Niah, two brothers who ruled the city together," Waif tells you. "They brought all manner of trees and palms to form a garden here, right in the center of Atraharsis."

Lines of bluish stones make up a broken path through the grove. You pass beneath half an arch, then come to a broken stone bench resting between the hollowed-out husks of two once magnificent trees. A headless statue stands nearby, holding a worn tablet. And on that tablet, etched in charcoal...

"Look! It's the symbol from Murdoch's journal!" You rush over to the statue. "He was here!" Beneath the symbol, scrawled in jagged black lettering:

Gold and red or you will be dead

Heed these words and live instead

"Grim..." Waif swallows. He looks around nervously. "What do you think it means?"

You both freeze uncomfortably, waiting for something terrible to happen. Nothing does. The screech of a bird reaches your ears from somewhere far away.

"I understand Murdoch's crews leaving messages for each other," Waif says. "But what's with all the rhymes?"

You shrug. "Robert Murdoch was eccentric but brilliant. No one's sure why he was such a weird guy."

"Hey!" Waif laughs merrily. "That rhymes!"

Punch Waif in the arm and continue on by *TURNING TO PAGE 18*

132

You step forward slowly, keeping your eyes peeled for signs of danger. The rest of the palace seems empty. There's nothing else here to find.

Eventually you approach the moaning face. With every step you take, things get a little more eerie. Finally you're on top of it. And that's when you realize the wall behind the face is broken and open to the street.

You chuckle. The moaning sound is nothing more than the wind blowing through the large ceramic mask. A glint of something else catches your eye. With your elbow, you shatter the lower half of the bearded man's jaw to reveal a small, secret niche. Still resting within the space you find a threadbare pouch of silver and gold coins!

"Here!" Waif catches the pouch as you throw it over to him. Coins spill into his palm and his eyes light up instantly.

"Any objection to holding *these*?" you ask.

"None!" Waif cries excitedly.

Good job, ummm... facing your fears?

Head back outside and *TURN TO PAGE 55*

You see the East Gate of Atraharsis long before you arrive there. Presiding over it is an enormous stone colossus. The statue might once have been magnificent, but is now so blasted by sand and sun it's almost entirely featureless. It's impossible to tell even if the figure was originally a man or a woman. Either way, it points with one broken arm into the city, in the direction of a long, slender tower.

"That's the Queen's Tower," you tell Waif. "According to Murdoch's map."

"I thought it was your uncle's map?"

"*Grand*-uncle," you explain again. "And yes. Err, I mean, no. I mean, he bought the map from someone who knew a guy whose second cousin was once married to a member of Murdoch's crew, so..."

Waif looks back at you utterly confused.

"Forget it. I'm sorry I said anything."

You turn your attention back to the entrance to the city. One of the tremendous iron-bound gates is still here, the rotted wood hanging from a monstrous hinge, half-buried in the sand. Just beyond that, the wide, sand-strewn avenues of Atraharsis lay spread out before you. After the cold desert night, the sun is starting to feel good on your back.

"We may need this," Waif says, pulling a torch from his pack. He lights it, and the flames drive away just that much more of the morning cold.

You have three choices of direction here.

You can head north, to where there seems to be some sort of movement in the early morning shadows. If so, *GO TO PAGE 90*

You can head west, toward what looks to be some sort of hole or well dug into the ground. *EXPLORE IT BY TURNING TO PAGE 82*

Finally you can head south, where the avenue appears to open into a broad, spacious area. *DO THAT ON PAGE 167*

134

The East Gate could still be a long distance away. If there's an easy way into the city right here, you figure you might as well explore it.

"Let me get a better look," Waif says. He drops his pack temporarily and starts climbing amongst the jagged stone. "It appears the tremors have opened a–"

Your friend's sentence is interrupted by a great sucking sound. The sand and stone shifts all around him, and before you can do anything Waif is sliding downward into what looks to be a giant sinkhole.

"Help!"

You're still on solid footing but you're losing your partner fast! You could rush down and grab him (giving up solid ground) or you could try to find some other way to rescue Waif. Time's running out though...

If you rush forward to grab Waif, *TURN TO PAGE 141*

If you'd rather sit tight and explore other options, *FLIP BACK TO PAGE 64*

You leave the Ziggurat behind you and enter the Grand Plaza. Dozens of palaces and two-story structures rise up to form a large community here. All of them are fancy and elaborate. You marvel at how beautiful everything is, even in utter ruin. A whole team of archaeologists could spend their entire lives here, and never get tired of their work.

"Up ahead," Waif indicates. "Look. The street."

The tremors have hit this part of the city especially hard. There are few structures left standing. What appears to be a large, jagged wall is actually the other half of the avenue, risen up out of the ground.

"See that?"

Beneath the broken avenue, a series of underground passages run beneath the city. As sunlight filters down you can see the walls are paved with smooth, clean stone.

"The undercity," you say excitedly. "This is what we want! This is where we'll find the Hall of Kings!"

Waif hops down. Casting one last glance up at Atraharsis, you follow him.

"Which way?"

The light of your partner's torch illuminates a long hall, which runs north and south. Both directions look identical in every way.

If you take the north passage, *GO TO PAGE 65*
If you'd rather go south instead, *HEAD TO PAGE 81*

136

You look at the blocks again and again. But no matter how long you stare at them, you still don't know which ones to use.

"Looks like you're climbing," you tell Waif.

Your partner rubs his hands with sand, stretches his fingers, and begins the ascent. At first it's slow going. Only the smallest cracks in the smooth marble of the column give Waif any potential hand or toeholds. Yet somehow, insanely, he still manages to climb his way up. He's halfway there, then three-quarters... and then finally he reaches the top.

"Waif!" you hiss. "Be careful!"

Slowly and delicately, Waif removes the glimmering green jewel from its mount. Then he slides back down the column, hugging the marble with his entire body to keep from slipping too fast.

"That was amazing!" you tell him when he's back on his feet. You almost can't even believe it. "You're incredible!"

"I am Waif," he grins. He holds out his hand and drops the jewel into your palm, where it shines with a radiance all its own. It's the single most beautiful thing you've ever seen.

Congratulations! You've recovered the star emerald of Atraharsis!

Somewhere off in the distance, a dust cloud swirls on the desert horizon. You squint into it, but can't make out any details.

"Let's get of here," you tell Waif. Together, you make your way down the steps and out of the Queen's Tower.

———————————— ◉ ————————————

Nice work getting the jewel! But can you keep it?
HEAD ON OVER TO PAGE 116

The rumbling gets louder. The tremors get more violent. Waif yells something over the chaos, but you can't hear him.

The giant chunk of stone hurtles downward. It's coming straight for you! There's no time to avoid it!

A sunburst of white sparks explodes somewhere in the back of your vision, then everything goes black...

Yikes. Did you really roll a 3? Tough one. Are you *sure* you didn't roll something else?

Well, okay. Maybe next time you'll do better. But for now, as premature as it seems, this is going to be

---

THE END

138

You bring your hand down violently on Waif's forearm. It flings the scorpion upward, high into the air. You both watch as it goes sailing across the room, tumbling end over end before landing and skittering away. Together you look back at Waif's hand...

There's not a single mark on it.

"Wow," Waif breathes. "That was... quick thinking."

"Yeah," you tell him. "You're welcome. Now let's pick the *right* lense this time."

If you try the red lense *GO BACK TO PAGE 26*
If you go with the yellow lense *TURN TO PAGE 37*

"My grand-uncle spent his whole life hoping to get to this place," you say. "So let's be thorough."

The two of you get to work searching the area. It's mostly dirt and rubble, but you find scraps of other wood and fabric buried beneath the sands. The place was once a city square, as far as you can figure. A place where vendors set up small shops and sold their wares.

You're about to give up and move on when Waif produces a small piece of pottery. As he lifts it the bottom drops out, spilling a cascade of tiny shimmering globes into the sand.

"Pearls!" he cries out excitedly.

You kneel to help him gather up the tiny treasures. There are at least a hundred of them in all, from black to lavender to milky white.

"Truly this is a city of riches," Waif breathes.

"Maybe," you say, holding up one of the larger pearls. "It's still not a star jewel though." Your eyes are drawn upward to the distant tower. At the top, something green glints in the rising sun.

Not a bad start!

Now continue along the northern avenue by *TURNING TO PAGE 85*

140

The ants are swarming. Churning. They form an semi-circle at your feet, their bodies rolling beneath the sun in a red, deadly wave.

"Waif!" you cry out. "Your torch!"

Gripped by panic, it seems your partner has forgotten all about his firebrand. He brandishes now, swinging it down and forward. A few ants fall beneath the flames, but there are way too many. The torch just isn't enough.

"Hang on..."

You unsling your rucksack and reach inside. For one panicked moment you think you left it back at camp, but then your hand closes around the object of your search: a small metal cannister of lamp oil.

Quickly you squirt the oil onto the cobbles, creating a curved line separating you and Waif from the advancing army of ants. Eventually the container goes empty and you toss it. You can only hope it's enough.

"Light it!"

Waif does as he's told. The flammable liquid goes up instantly, igniting in a huge wave of heat and smoke. You hear a distinct crackle as the front line of ants falls victim to the flames. The ants just behind them fall back and retreat.

"It's working!" you shout triumphantly. But you also know it won't last forever. You and Waif will need to get moving before the flames die down, or before reinforcements arrive. You grab his shoulder and pull him backward, away from the battle.

"Which way? East or west?"

If you'd like to go east, *FLIP ALL THE WAY BACK TO PAGE 13*
If you'd rather go west, *HEAD OVER TO PAGE 82*

"Waif, quick! Grab my hand!"

Sprinting forward without thinking, you extend your arm. Your partner reaches back, and then suddenly you're *both* sliding into the sinkhole!

Sand rushes past you. It fills your ears, your mouth, your nose... Somehow you stay on top, doing your best to avoid the rock and rubble tumbling past to fill the gaping hole. The sand-slide begins to slow, and then eventually, stops altogether. You're buried up to your waist in the newly-shifted desert. It takes you a good minute or two to pull yourself free.

"Waif! WAIF!"

Your voice echoes against the empty horizon. There's no answer. Your friend is gone, buried beneath the sands of Atraharsis.

You hardly knew him, but you're overcome with a profound sense of sorrow and loss. Unwilling to face the city alone, you reluctantly accept that this is

THE END

142

You stand in what appears to be a large, circular chamber. But as the torchlight reaches the walls, it's revealed the room is actually hexagonal. Each of the sides contain a single arched exit. And above each shadowy opening–

"Look! The glyphs!"

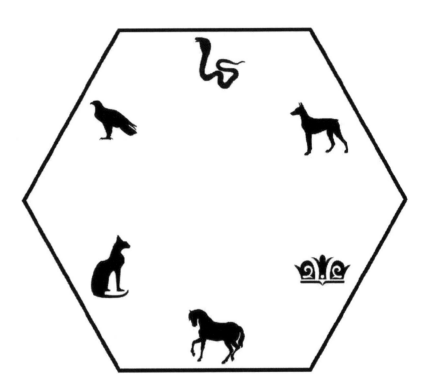

Six images are carved deeply into the stone, one directly above each opening. You spin in a circle, examining all of them.

"One of these leads to the Hall of Kings," you tell Waif. "It just *has* to..."

You stare at the openings. They all look the same. Each is completely identical to all the others, except for the different markings carved overhead.

Alright, this is it! Make your choice!

If you choose the exit marked with the SERPENT, take a really deep breath and *GO TO PAGE 117*

If you pick the exit marked with the DOG, swallow once and *HEAD OVER TO PAGE 146*

If you pick the exit marked with the CROWN, deliver a very royal salute and *TURN TO PAGE 99*

If you pick the exit marked with the HORSE, let out a long, deep breath and *FLIP BACK TO PAGE 20*

If you pick the exit marked with the CAT, try to land on your feet *OVER ON PAGE 156*

If you pick the exit marked with the HAWK, see what happens when you *TURN TO PAGE 160*

144

"Jump!" Waif screams. He's nearly drowned completely out by the thunder of the surging river. "Do it NOW!"

There's no time to line things up or even hesitate – all you can do get in motion. You take your best running start, plant your left foot against the lip of the receding floor, and launch yourself toward the opposite hallway.

You sail forward, feeling the powerful rush of air churning beneath you. Waif looks so small, so very far away. Your foot catches something... and then suddenly you're through the opening. You made it!

"I... can't... believe..."

You fall. Not into the river, though. This time the floor of the hallway gives out, dropping you through a chute and along a rough stone ramp. You bang up against Waif a few times, and then the both of you are ejected – through the ceiling – into another large chamber.

For a few moments you just lie there, dizzy from the fall, grateful to be alive. Then you pick yourself up, check for broken bones, and help Waif to his feet.

Where'd you end up now? Find out when you *FLIP BACK TO PAGE 142*

Here the street doubles back upon itself, creating a wide avenue that skirts the northernmost reaches of the city. Not far in the distance, the Queens Tower looms against the morning sky. Its smooth, almost-reflective surface curves inward as it juts upward from the sands, creating a feminine, hourglass shape.

Standing between you and the tower, a raised pavilion is set off to one side. A series of beautifully carved marble columns are set equidistant from one another in a large rectangle.

"As much as I want that tower," you say, pointing upward, "this is too interesting not to check it out." Waif nods his agreement, and moments later, you're at the top of a small set of granite steps.

The floor here is clean, the debris minimal. A series of large, elongated stones – pieces of the toppled columns – lay strewn about, the edges polished smooth by centuries beneath the shifting sands. Kneeling before one, you're attempting to read an inscription at the base when, all of a sudden, Waif starts backing up in your direction.

"What's the–"

Then you see it. Ahead of you, crawling forward on all fours, is an enormous, razor-toothed monitor lizard. The creature is freakishly huge – maybe twice the size of a Komodo Dragon – all scales and claws and muscle. Its thick pink tongue flicks in and out of its mouth as it sniffs the air.

"Waif..." you whisper, as if somehow lowering your voice might help. He doesn't move. "Waif!"

Waif stands beside you, frozen against one of the rounded white stones. There are three more such stones behind you. You grab the only weapon you have – your camping hatchet – and wield it with as much ferocity as you can. Which to be honest, isn't much.

With the monster still advancing, it's time to make your move.

If you decide to fighting the lizard is your best bet, *TURN TO PAGE 77*

If you'd rather hide behind the set of large stones, *TRY THAT OPTION ON PAGE 56*

Or maybe you can just yank Waif out of the way and make a break for it. If so, *GO TO PAGE 111*

146

You look at the glyph shaped like a dog. Innocent and pure. Man's best friend.

"The dog looks good," you say. After all, what could go wrong?

Together you pass beneath the glyph and enter a dark corridor. You haven't gone more than a few dozen steps when, suddenly–

"The floor!" Waif cries. "It's rising up behind us!"

You whirl around. The floor you just crossed is tilting upward, turning the entire corridor into a steep incline. By the time you turn back it's already too late – your legs buckle. The torch goes out. Waif lets out a scream and you find yourself sliding downward, into the oblivion of utter darkness.

"Unnffff!"

You fall and fall, yet somehow when you land you're still alive. Waif re-ignites the torch and you find yourselves in a high-slung cavern, sprawled across an enormous pile of sand. The walls are rough-hewn, scarred by the blades of a thousand primitive tools. The ceiling stretches high overhead.

"The quarry," Waif says. You notice an ominous tone in his voice. "The founders excavated here to build the city. These tunnels... they go on for miles and miles."

There must be a dozen exits from this room alone. All of them are pitch black. As if reading your mind, Waif follows your gaze to the torch. How many hours of light are left? How much water is still in your canteens?

There are thousands of tunnels that make up the maze down here. Maybe you'll be able to navigate them. Maybe you'll be able to make it out.

Or maybe all the exits collapsed in on themselves thousands of years ago. You don't know the answers to these questions, but ultimately you'll find out.

For now however, this appears to be

THE END

The simple stone staircase empties unceremoniously into the second level of the Queen's Tower. This floor is even more lavish than the first. The furnishings are more preserved, the walls more brightly painted. The staircase you arrived at continues upward, spiraling high along the wall. It appears to go past a few more missing floors, all the way to the top.

Shining down from the upper opening is a gleaming green light.

"The star emerald!" Waif cries eagerly. Immediately he starts up the staircase... until you place a hand on his shoulder.

"Hang on," you say. "It was an effort just getting to the tower. Let's not go running around too fast."

Your partner steps down reluctantly. Together you search the second floor. There's not much here, but at least everything doesn't crumble to the touch.

You're about to set foot on the steps again when Waif calls you over. "Come. Look at this."

He's standing over a moldy chest. Your partner has already brushed the sand aside and gotten it open. Inside is a smaller object made of delicate green glass.

"Should we touch it?" he asks. Instead of answering him you pick it up. You turn it over in your hands a few times before realizing what it is.

"It's a puzzle box!"

"A what?"

"A puzzle box. My grand-uncle had a few of them. They're always different, but he taught me a few tricks on how to solve them." The crystalline structure of the box is sleek and beautiful. You can see there's something inside, but refraction from the glass makes it impossible to tell what it is.

"I'll bet I can open it," you tell Waif.

If you'd like to give the box a try, roll two dice (or just pick a random number from 2 to 12)

If the roll comes up odd, *TURN TO PAGE 79*

If the roll comes up even, *TURN TO PAGE 23*

Or maybe you'd like to put the box in your rucksack and continue upward. If so, *GO TO PAGE 122*

148

You move to the lever at the western side of the room. You figure one door's as good as the other.

"Waif, help me pull."

The lever comes down with the smooth ease of good engineering. The granite block begins to lower, while simultaneously, a door rises out of the floor in the west side passage. Even when the mechanism is fully raised, you realize it hasn't blocked much sun.

"Maybe if we—"

"Aaahhhh!"

Something large and dark leaps from the top of the ancient counterweight. Disturbed from its resting place, a huge spider lunges at Waif!

Roll a single die (or just pick a random number from 1 to 6)

If the number is a 1 or 6, *TURN TO PAGE 108*

If the number is a 2, 3, 4 or 5, *GO TO PAGE 70*

Left, right... one random hallway is as good as another. You split the difference and take the center.

The light from Waif's torch reveals crude stone walls wet with condensation. They seem to grow darker the further you go. At one point the corridor makes a U-turn, doubling back on itself, and that's when things get significantly steeper.

"Careful," you tell Waif as the floor curves even further downward. He starts to respond when his foot skids on a patch of sand!

You reach for your friend as he slips over the edge. He's light. It should be an easy catch... but as you grab for him your own feet slide out from under you on the sandy incline. Together you fall, skidding downward, trying to avoid the burning torch along the way. Ultimately you're deposited into another room, dropped rudely through a hole in the chamber's ceiling.

"Ugh," you groan as you rise slowly to your feet. "I've almost had enough of this place."

Waif's raises his torch and his eyes go wide. "Almost..."

Ouch! You're gonna feel that in the morning. Now *TURN TO PAGE 142*

150

"Forget it," you shout to Waif. "Just run!"

You turn your backs to the wave of insects and start running. Waif is just ahead of you. The ants are swarming behind you, surging forward. You can hear the rustling of their carapaces as they slide against and climb over each other.

There's a brief, heart-stopping moment when you're sure they've caught you. You can actually feel the creatures crawling up your feet, skittering beneath your pants leg, biting you in the calves... But the pain never comes. Either it's all in your head, or you're too numb to feel it. You want to turn around, to see if you've beaten them. But as Waif glances back over his own shoulder, the fear in his eyes tells you not to.

Finally Waif slows, mere seconds before it feels like your heart is going to explode. You take it down to a jog, then a walk. When you finally look back you see only a dozen or so ants left in the street, crawling in mindless circles.

"That... was... close..." you breathe. "I... I don't..."

"Take it easy," Waif tells you. "We're safe." Not only hasn't he broken a sweat, he isn't even out of breath! You don't know whether to be angry or jealous.

You rest until your breath comes back, helped along by a cool drink from your friend's canteen. When you look up, the avenue you're on has reached a junction point. One road heads east into the rising sun. The other stretches in the opposite direction.

If you'd like to go east, *TURN TO PAGE 13*
If you'd rather go west, *FLIP TO PAGE 82*

Your legs shake as the floor grumbles beneath your feet. Frantically you look down. Sand is scattered in small piles around you.

Earth is key...

"Waif!" you cry. "Help me gather some sand!"

Cupping your hands together, you start scooping up sand and dumping it into the altar. As expected, it runs straight out of the holes on all four sides. But something else happens too. The floor seems to be slowing down.

"Keep going!"

You both alternate, taking turns scooping and loading the altar with sand. As you develop a rhythm the floor slows its ascent even more. But it still doesn't stop...

Waif's hand closes over your shoulder as he suddenly points upward. "Look!"

A number of stones have retracted, creating a hole in the ceiling. There's a glyph carved beside the opening you hadn't seen before.

"Water!" Waif translates. "Water, life!"

Waif drags you over until you're standing directly beneath the hole. Arms at your sides, the two of you hold your breath as you're pushed upward, straight through the new opening. The floor slams into the ceiling with a dull *BOOM*, knocking you right to your knees.

"Here!"

When you look up again, you're in the equivalent of a stone cylinder with no roof. Waif has already climbed out. He extends a hand downward and pulls you into the upper chamber.

Pretty slick escape! *NOW TURN TO PAGE 142*

152

You continue along the shadowy corridors until they spill you into a long, narrow hallway. The floor is different here. Instead of the smooth mortared flagstone you've been walking on the entire time, this floor is made up of square clay tiles.

"Hang on," you say as Waif moves to step into the hall. "Something's up here."

Holding the torch low, you can see the tiles come in three colors: white, black, and red. They seem randomly distributed along the length of the hall in no distinguishable pattern.

"We have to go through here," your partner shrugs. He points to a dark exit at the opposite end. "There's no other way."

Looks like you'll need to tread carefully. Lift your leg and make a choice:

If you step on a white tile, *TURN TO PAGE 170*

If you step on a black tile, *TURN TO PAGE 61*

If you step on a red tile, *TURN TO PAGE 113*

You push your palm against the obelisk key and begin to turn counter-clockwise. The stone shifts beneath your hand...

"Wait!"

Waif's hand slaps itself over your wrist. You stop.

"The *right* way is NOT the left!" he exclaims. "That means you should turn it to the right!"

You pause in confusion for a moment, and then the answer hits you. Waif's right! Whew! Good thing he's here.

Turn the obelisk key to the right *BY GOING TO PAGE 47*

154

You continue on through the darkness (who would've thought?) feeling your way around the room. As you explore the area for some sort of way out, you find the chamber you're in is little more than a great big cave.

"Look," Waif says. "Stuff."

A heap of old tapestries is the only indication of human presence down here. They rest in a large, rotting pile, so far gone it's impossible to tell what they once represented.

"Do you think the–"

Waif stops talking as something shifts in the darkness. A smell washes over the room. It's a powerful earthy smell, all mold and funk and putrescence.

"Watch out!"

Like something out of a living nightmare, an enormous subterranean slug looms over you. Somehow, down here in the darkness, the creature has grown to gargantuan proportions. Its tentacles probe the air blindly, reaching for something. Anything...

If you've picked up something to use against the giant slug, use the chart below to add up all the letters in that word. Once you have the total, you can *GO TO THAT PAGE.*

A = 1	F = 6	K = 11	P = 16	U = 21	Z = 26
B = 2	G = 7	L = 12	Q = 17	V = 22	Example:
C = 3	H = 8	M = 13	R = 18	W = 23	ANNA =
D = 4	I = 9	N = 14	S = 19	X = 24	1+14+14+1
E = 5	J = 10	O = 15	T = 20	Y = 25	= 30

If you don't have anything, you'll have to fight the slug off! Roll two dice (or just pick a random number from 2 to 12).

If the total of your roll is 7 or lower, *TURN TO PAGE 35*

If the total of your roll is 8 or higher, *TURN TO PAGE 168*

"I'm not guessing which gems go where," you say. "Let's just take the left hallway."

Waif casts a hungry look back at the jewel-studded wall, but still doesn't protest. Together you enter the leftmost corridor. As you walk side by side into the darkness, the air gets colder. The walls take on moisture as well.

All of a sudden Waif halts. "Wait," he says warily. "I think I heard something."

"Heard what?"

"I'm not sure. Some kind of–"

BOOM!

An ear-splitting crash precedes a gargantuan stone block dropping straight down from the ceiling. It lands a mere six feet in front of you, sending up a plume of grey dust and totally blocking the way.

"Donovan! You okay?"

A chill rockets through your body, causing the hairs on your arms and neck to stand on end. If your partner hadn't stopped when he did, you'd be a pancake right now.

"Uhhh... thanks?" Even in the orange torchlight you're pretty sure you're white as a ghost.

Waif puts a consoling hand on your shoulder and turns you gently around. "Let's pick another hallway."

You can take the hallway on the right *BY GOING TO PAGE 68*
Or you can take the center hallway *OVER ON PAGE 149*

156

You look from one glyph to the other. At first glance they all look the same. But there has to be something. Something to distinguish the one right answer from the five wrong ones...

"Wait!" You practically throw your rucksack from your back. Waif watches as you rifle through it and produce your grand-uncle's journal.

"Remember what it said on the back of the map?" you cry. You find the page and flip it over. "Here: 'It takes *nine lives* to find the Hall of Kings'."

Waif still looks confused. "So?"

"The cat! That's what Murdoch meant!" You point up at the smooth curves of the feline glyph. "The *cat's* the one who has nine lives!"

Your partner's face curls into a sly grin as it finally sinks in. One by one he points to the other openings. "From six less five..."

"Exactly!"

Shuddering with excitement, you pass beneath the cat glyph. The hall is simple, undecorated. It ends in a plain stone door, covered with more glyphs.

"They're names," Waif says. "The names of all those who ruled Atraharsis."

Just as he finishes his sentence a hollow boom echoes from somewhere deep below. The door grinds open. Centuries of dust and dirt fall away, revealing more darkness.

The torchlight flickers, probably because Waif's arm is shaking. Silently you take it from him and hold it out before you.

"Come on," you say. And without another word you disappear into the wide, sweeping chamber...

The room is enormous. It goes on for as far as you can see. Light flares as Waif ignites a second torch from his pack. Suddenly the illumination is reflected everywhere... by polished shields, glimmering jewels, and long stacks of gleaming gold!

You found it! The Hall of Kings!

158

"I... I don't belie–"

"Oh you'd *better* believe it!" you cry exuberantly. The slap on the back you give him almost knocks Waif over. "We're finally here!"

You practically dance down the center of the enormous hall. Tall statues line both sides, beautifully carved in the likeness of men and women. The rulers of Atraharsis, you realize. The founders, the scholars, the kings and queens. All of them are here, preserved in marble, their names and deeds engraved on stone tablets beneath their feet.

And that's not all. Each king and queen has been honored in other ways too, as gifts from the people of their reign litter the floor around each statue. You see coins, gems, jars of spices and incense. Idols of gold and silver, ivory and jade. Chests overflow with totems and trinkets. Waif picks up a jeweled dagger, chased with precious metals. You blow the dust from something nearby, and a diamond-studded tiara is revealed.

The walls behind each ruler are set with mosaics and other great works of art, presumably spinning tales of the highlights of their life. There's more than you could ever take, or carry, or even spend. It's overwhelming, yet humbling at the same time.

"This... this is crazy," you say. "I don't know what else to say."

Waif places a bag of jewels in your hand, each one so big and perfect it doesn't even look real. "Say you'll take what you need," he tells you, "to save your grand-uncle's estate. Say you'll honor his memory, as the people of Atraharsis honored the memory of their own ancestors."

You nod quietly. Once again you find yourself wishing your grand-uncle could be here. Perhaps he is, you think fondly. At least in spirit.

Waif's voice breaks you from your thoughts. "Donovan. Come over here." At the other end of the room, a simple pedestal rests against the far wall. Waif is huddled over it, pointing to a series of glyphs just above.

"What does it say?" you ask.

Waif translates: "*Place here man's greatest treasure.*"

There's silence in the room as you pause, considering.

"Greatest treasure?" Waif repeats. He glances around the room. "That could be *anything*. I mean, just look at all of this!"

You rub your chin. "Or maybe it means something else," you say.

"Like what?" All of a sudden Waif's eyes light up. "Water!" he cries. "We're in the desert, maybe the greatest treasure is water?"

"Could be," you allow. Your friend stops in the middle of grabbing his canteen.

"Life?" Waif offers. "After all the danger we've been through, maybe man's greatest treasure is life itself?"

His new answer sounds better, but still you're not so sure. How could you put 'life' on the tiny pedestal? It must be something else...

Do you have the answer? If you know man's greatest treasure, use the chart below to add up all the letters in that word. Once you have the total, you can *GO TO THAT PAGE*

A = 1	F = 6	K = 11	P = 16	U = 21	Z = 26
B = 2	G = 7	L = 12	Q = 17	V = 22	Example:
C = 3	H = 8	M = 13	R = 18	W = 23	ANNA =
D = 4	I = 9	N = 14	S = 19	X = 24	1+14+14+1
E = 5	J = 10	O = 15	T = 20	Y = 25	= 30

If you don't know it, you can always try something else. Offer up another treasure by *GOING TO PAGE 165*

160

For some reason you have a good feeling about the hawk glyph. "Let's take that one."

Passing beneath the great bird you walk a dark corridor for what seems like a very long time. The floor feels like it slopes upward in the darkness, or maybe it's just your imagination.

"This doesn't seem right," you wonder aloud. "I think–"

You're rocked as the ground beneath you suddenly shakes. Dust and debris crumble from the ceiling, filling your eyes, shrouding your vision as the rumble grows to an almost deafening roar.

Waif points frantically upward. "Light!" Sure enough, sunlight streams in from several cracks in the masonry above. Then a tremendous rushing sound drowns out everything else, and you're being flung down the corridor by a torrent of icy cold water.

"The river!"

Darkness swallows you as the torch is snuffed out. You can't fight it. There's nothing to do but keep your head up as you roll with the churning, swirling rapids. Thankfully, the river isn't pulling you down. It's pushing you up instead, faster and faster, until you crash hard against the ceiling and break through, into the blinding light of the desert sun.

Atraharsis is behind you... but the city is sinking! A cloud of dust swirls high into the air as the broken walls and towers are once again swallowed beneath the sands. You and Waif are deposited on the bank of a temporary oasis, by waters that recede even as you stumble to your feet. Eventually you're left standing at the edge of a rubble-strewn field. Only a few scattered pieces of marble and sandstone give the slightest indication that a city once stood here.

Waif is the first to break the silence. "I wonder if we made the right choice?"

You think of your lost star gem, and the other star jewels that you missed. About all the treasures hidden throughout the city, and of course, the Hall of Kings. "No," you tell him. "I'm pretty sure we messed up."

Lying in the sand nearby you notice your rucksack. At least you still have that, and whatever other valuables you may have found. It might not be enough to save your grand-uncle's estate, but you also have the most important treasure of all: your life.

As you lift your pack the obelisk key rolls out. It stares up at you playfully from the sand.

"Come on Waif," you smile. "Looks like Atraharsis is done with us... for today at least."

THE END

162

Waif points to a door that wasn't there before. Beyond it you find a tunnel, long and straight and ending in a patch of blue sky. The walls shake as you sprint down its length, holding your breath against plumes of thick, choking dust. A good part of one wall caves in right in front of you, but you manage to hurdle it without breaking stride.

There's one last violent tremor and then you're through; the tunnel spits you out into the desert, to bake beneath a blazing yellow sun. You want to flop down in exhaustion. But as Waif pulls you free of the opening, past the broken remnants of the hidden door, he points backward. "Look! The city!"

Somehow you're already beyond the shattered city walls. Yet Waif is still tugging you along, ushering you frantically in the opposite direction. And then you see why:

Atraharsis is sinking.

Long, sweeping dunes collapse around it as the city is sucked beneath the desert floor. You watch it all go – every wall, every stone, every shattered home and palace. As the last of the broken towers are swallowed a great cloud forms in the air overhead. It looks like the sandstorm you encountered last night, only much thicker and a lot more concentrated. The ground still rumbles beneath you. The sand still shifts under your feet.

When the dust clears you're standing on the edge of a bleak, barren plain. Broken bits of marble and cracked sandstone are the only indications that anything once stood here. A few hours from now, these too will be swallowed by the dunes themselves.

"Back where it belongs," Waif says solemnly. "The city beneath the sands."

You stand there for a long while, just staring back at the void where Atraharsis used to be. Then it's time to go. Climbing back up the cliff face is hard, especially in the mid-day sun with canteens that are nearly empty. But you make it. You make it all the way back to your camp, when all of a sudden...

"*Young!*"

You whirl at the sound of a gruff voice. Standing between you and your tent is the hulking, mustached form of John Sullivan.

"What was all that?" he demands. The big adventurer is flanked by another two men. They're both as sun-bronzed as him, but not nearly as huge.

"What was what?"

His face goes sour. "Don't give me that! The rumbling! The shaking! All those tremors – don't tell me you didn't hear any of that!"

Slowly you turn toward Waif. His face is the picture of innocence. "Did *you* hear anything?" you ask him.

"No," Waif says. "Not that I recall."

Sullivan goes red. He scans your campsite, which at this point is nothing more than a few smoldering coals and single tent shredded by last night's storm. "Well what the heck have you been doing up here?"

You give a casual shrug. "We were going to have a breakfast, actually," you say. "A bit late, but if you wanted to–"

"Forget it!" Sullivan cries. His mouth curls into a snarl. "Looks like you're done here anyway. Have been for a while." He turns to stomp off. Before he does, his eyes shift to your partner.

"C'mon Waif," he spits. "We need every man today, so I guess you're–"

"No." The word is firm. Unmistakable. But from the look of confusion on Sullivan's face, you'd think Waif was speaking an entirely different language.

"Did you just say *no?*"

"Yeah," you say, stepping forward. "He did." You stand tall now, beside your friend. "Oh, and one more thing. His name's not 'Waif'. It's *Renn.*"

Sullivan's eyes flare. He almost says something... almost, but not quite. Then he shakes his head and storms away. You watch silently until he and his men disappear over the next ridge.

"Thanks," Waif says. His voice is low now. Choked up and full of emotion. But you shake your head at him.

"No," you tell him. "I should be the one thanking *you.* None of this would've happened without your help. I would've never found Atraharsis, or the Hall of Kings. I would've never recovered the star jewel. Or rather, *almost* recovered it..."

164

Waif smiles. You can't help but notice it's a weird smile, though.

"Yeah..." he says. "About that..."

One hand fishes into his pocket. When it comes out, he's holding the star jewel. It's even more beautiful in the sun. Blinding, even.

You just stand there. Dumbstruck.

"What! I... I... *HOW?*"

Waif holds out the jewel and drops it into your hand. It takes up your entire palm. He turns sideways, gesturing with one hand to accentuate how small and thin he actually is.

"You're right," he says. "I *am* Renn. But sometimes, it's good to be Waif too..."

You found gold, gems, treasure. You located the Hall of Kings, won a star jewel, and recovered the long-lost knowledge of Atraharsis.

CONGRATULATIONS!
YOU HAVE REACHED THE ULTIMATE ENDING!

In recognition for taking up the gauntlet, let it be known to fellow adventurers that you are hereby granted the title of:

Adventurer Extraordinaire!

You may go here: **www.ultimateendingbooks.com/extras.php** and enter code

ST17490

for tons of extras, and to print out your Ultimate Ending Book One certificate!

And for a special sneak peek of Ultimate Ending Book 2, *JUMP TO PAGE 171*

"Maybe it just wants our biggest treasure," you say, "before allowing us to leave. You know, as a kind of sacrifice."

Waif scans the chamber again as if seeing it for the first time. "You could be right," he says. "Now that you mention it, I don't see any sign of an exit anywhere."

Together you search for the best possible offering. You settle on a magnificent scepter of gold, studded with sapphires, rubies, and emeralds. It must've belonged to someone very important. One of the more beloved rulers of Atraharsis.

"Here we go." Gingerly you lay the jeweled rod on the plain stone altar. An area beneath the object begins to sink, lowering the scepter smoothly into the floor.

You wait. For an agonizing minute, nothing occurs. Then a series of noises begins – hollow booms, deep in the earth, far beneath your feet.

A door opens. Light streams in. You see a tunnel that slants upward for a long while... and a second door near the top, open to the sky.

"That was it!" Waif cries. "We did it!"

Quickly you gather your things. Each of you brings a hand-picked array of treasure, and you take a few moments to stuff it securely in your packs. While you do, the noises beneath your feet continue. They grow louder in volume, until finally the Hall itself starts to rumble.

"Let's go," you say sternly. "Now."

Rocks and debris begin to shake from the ceiling, filling the hall with plumes of cascading dust. The two of you run for the exit. You stop to look back one last time on the grandeur of the Hall of Kings, willing your brain to emblazon this moment so you can enjoy it for the rest of your life.

The ground shakes as you race down the tunnel. It's long – longer than it first looked – and in a moment's panic you wonder if you'll make it in time. You imagine the irony of losing everything at the very end, but then you break free, hurtling past the once-hidden opening and into a world of sun and azure sky.

166

You look up and are surprised to find yourself beyond the city walls. Sand rushes down from two different hillsides in an avalanche of movement. It feels like the entire desert is shaking.

"Look!" Waif cries. "The city!"

Not far behind you, Atraharsis is sinking. You watch the buildings go, then the walls, then the broken minarets. You continue to scramble backward, throwing one arm over your eyes as the last tower is covered in sand. A swirling cloud of dust rolls over you, very much like the sandstorm that started it all. When the smoke clears, there's nothing left where a city once stood.

Waif doubles over in a fit of coughing. He looks grey from head to toe — you're both totally caked with dirt and dust. "The city beneath the sands," he finally says. "Gone again."

You heft your rucksack with one hand. It's pleasantly heavy. "Gone but not forgotten," you chime in. Waif laughs, and together you turn in the direction of your camp.

A smile paints its way across your face as you walk back. Aside from a few scrapes and bruises, you made it out virtually unscathed. Best of all you fulfilled your grand-uncle's lifelong dream. His estate will be safe now, his legacy secured for generations to come.

"You know," Waif says, pointing at the distant obelisk. "I wouldn't mind trying for one of those star gems again. Not right now," he adds hastily, "but you know... someday...."

The obelisk key is a five-pound lump pressed into the small of your back. "Yeah, maybe," you say with a grin. "Someday..."

THE END

Very carefully, you and Waif begin picking your way through the streets of Atraharsis. The going is slow at first. Rock and rubble lay strewn everywhere; there's not a building in the city that hasn't lost a good portion of its structure to the ravages of time. Sand is everywhere as well. It's piled high against the city's pitted stone architecture, leaving sweeping dunes that rise and fall in most of the open areas.

"There's some sort of a square through there," you point out. Up ahead, through a dirt-choked alleyway, you can see a wide swath of worn cobbled road. "Let's see what it is."

You're leading your partner beneath the shadows of two very decrepit-looking buildings when you feel the ground begin to rumble. The rumble turns into a full-blown shake as the noise increases in volume, and plumes of dust begin rising from every visible surface.

"Get against the walls!" you shout.

Since the walls themselves are shaking this seems counterintuitive, but a little protection is better than none at all. Across from you, on the opposite side of the alley, Waif is huddled in a tight ball. There's a shifting, grinding noise, and then suddenly an enormous piece of the building comes loose!

Quick! Roll a single die! (Or just pick a random number from 1 to 6)

If the number comes up a 1 or 2, *GO TO PAGE 63*

If the number is a 3, *FLIP BACK TO PAGE 137*

If you roll a 4, 5, or a 6, *TURN TO PAGE 115*

168

"Waif!" you shout. "Ummm... your torch!"

Your partner is already waving the firebrand at the slug's massive body. It might feel the heat, but being down here for its entire life has rendered the creature totally blind.

Retreating along the corridor you came from is not an option. You'd only be trapped against the stone portcullis. All you can do is look for another exit, so you circle along the outer wall of the chamber. Waif keeps the slug at bay as your fingers dance in the darkness, searching for any kind of opening. Then...

"Wait... stop! Look OUT!"

You forgot about the tapestries! As you trip backward over the moldering pile, the slug shifts in your direction. The dust-caked fabric breaks your fall, but the last thing you see is the enormous slime-coated monstrosity slamming down on you.

A bit gross, but this is definitely

THE END

TREASURES OF THE FORGOTTEN CITY

There are too many blocks, too many combinations. Too much margin for error. Your gaze shifts back to the marble column.

"Think you can climb it?" you ask Waif. He nods. Sorta.

You step back as he gets to it. Remarkably, he makes solid progress. Waif's fingers and toes find minuscule cracks and fissures in the column's surface. In just a couple of minutes, he's halfway up.

"What's that?" he asks abruptly. You listen, but you don't hear anything. To your surprise, Waif slides back down the column. He cocks his head curiously, then his eyes go wide and he heads for the staircase.

"RUN!"

There's no time to ask questions. With a last reluctant look toward the star emerald, you fly down the steps after your friend. It's not until you reach the second floor that you hear it. Or rather, you *feel* it...

The Queen's Tower is shaking.

A rumble begins somewhere beneath you. It grows louder and louder as the floor trembles. In no time, the Tower fills with dust. Chunks of stone break free from the walls, creating deadly projectiles that cartwheel downward all around you.

Waif keeps glancing back to see where you are. His eyes urge you to hurry. At long last you reach the bottom, where the two of you go flying out of the Tower entrance. You run far out into the street, not stopping until you're several blocks away.

CRASH!

From a safe vantage point, you and Waif watch the strange yet beautiful sight of the Queen's Tower collapsing in upon itself. A wave of harmless dust rolls over you both, and then you're staring at nothing but a large pile of rubble.

"That thing stood for four thousand years," you say with as serious a face as possible. "And you knocked it down in only ten minutes."

Waif looks back at you horrified. "But I... I didn't..." He stops only when you break out laughing.

"Relax," you tell him with a pat on the back. "There are still two other jewels in this city to go after."

Glad you're okay, but let's try not to destroy any more pieces of ancient history.
TURN TO PAGE 131

170

You decide to try a white tile. Gingerly you press down on it with your foot... and nothing happens.

"White's safe," you guess. "Let's try red."

You step on a red tile. Then a black one. There's no reaction at all. You can't help but feel silly. The whole thing is nothing more than a fancy tiled corridor.

"Well that was anti-climatic," you tell Waif. "Let's go."

The torchlight bounces gently as the two of you make your way toward the opposite end of the hall. You're about halfway down when...

CLICK!

"What was that?" you ask nervously.

"I– I'm not sure," Waif says. "All I did was step on this white tile and–"

A grinding noise erupts from your left and right, followed by a loud hissing sound. The room begins filling with–

"SAND!"

Dozens of small doors have opened in the walls on both sides of the hallway. Sand pours in from all directions. It piles rapidly all around you.

"Quick, Waif!" you shout. "Get back to the–"

You can't hear him. You can't see him. Everything is swallowed by darkness as Waif and his torch are swept beneath several tons of cool desert sand. You stumble backward in the blackness, trying to feel your way along the wall until you can no longer move.

Your feet are buried. Then your knees. You struggle against the rising sand, hoping for a miracle but realizing this is probably

THE END

SNEAK PEEK

Welcome to the House on Hollow Hill!

You are MIKE THOMPSON, a teenager in upstate New York. You're walking down the street with your friends Emma and Jake, admiring the autumn leaves on the trees lining the neighborhood.

Jake lets out a big sigh. "Let's go back to the field," he says, tossing a baseball back and forth with himself. "I want to practice my curveball."

Emma laughs. "You're the only kid who spends all day at school and wants to go back for more."

"I don't want to go back to *school,* I want to go back to the field *outside* of the school." He turns to you. "Come on Mike, you promised you'd play catch."

You shake your head at him. "I'll play catch with you this weekend. I need to get home and practice the piano." You have a test for music class tomorrow.

Jake sighs dramatically. "That's not what you promised."

"Leave off, Jake," Emma says. "I'm in Mrs. Baramule's class and have to practice too. She's strict! Can you believe she failed my sister for confusing a C with a C-sharp?" She rolled her eyes to let you know what she thought about *that.*

"Fine. But the next time you need help with anything..."

172

The massive house on the corner, old and decrepit, looms over you. "I heard old Mr. Goosen is moving out," you say.

Emma says, "Wow. He's lived in that house his whole life."

"He looks like he's lived there an entire *century,*" Jake says.

Suddenly there is a voice behind you. "Most of a century, in fact!" says Mr. Goosen. You whirl to face him and he smiles. He's wearing a tweed jacket on top of overalls, and his white hair hangs down his back. "Eighty-one years, to be exact."

Jake looks embarrassed, but you grin. Mr. Goosen has always been nice to you. "Is it true?" you ask. "You and your wife are going to move out?"

"We already have," he says, staring up at the massive three-story house. He shoves his hands in his pockets and looks strangely sad. "All that's left are things I can't take with me."

"Can't take with you?" Jake asks. "You mean you've left stuff inside the house? For anyone?"

"Yes, there's still plenty left in the house. I have too much stuff, you know, from all my adventures. I don't know what will happen to it all, now." Mr. Goosen is a well-known traveler: African safaris, scaling the Himalayas. He's done it all!

"You must be sad to leave so much," Emma says.

"Not at all," he replies. "The most important things are the memories! Got them all up here." He taps the side of his head.

Jake frowns with concentration. "Well if you're not taking them, and you don't know what's going to happen to them..."

"Jake!" Emma yells.

Mr. Goosen breaks out in a big smile. "Actually, that's exactly what I wanted to talk to you about..."

"I have one daughter and four grandkids, and they've already taken what they wanted. Everything else is going to be destroyed!"

"Destroyed?" Emma asks.

"The person who bought my house wants to build a new one," he says. "They're going to bulldoze the old one and everything inside." Mr. Goosen looks stricken by the thought.

"That's terrible!" you say.

Mr. Goosen points at you. "Yes, it is. I'd hate for everything to go to waste... so how would you like to keep something from inside? As a thank you for always being such good neighborhood kids?"

"Yeah!" Jake blurts out. He suddenly looks suspicious, and begins rolling his baseball between his fingers. "What's the catch?"

"No catch at all, son," Mr. Goosen says. "You three can go inside and take something before the bulldozers come."

"When are the bulldozers coming?" you ask.

"First thing tomorrow morning. So you have plenty of time."

Plenty of time? You and Emma have to practice for your music test! You both look at one-another. "Maybe if we just take a quick look..." Emma says.

"Oh, so you won't throw the ball at me, but you'll explore Mr. Goosen's house!" Jake says.

"You mean you don't want to go inside?" you ask.

Jake's frown turns into a toothy grin. "Okay, you got me. Of course I do!"

"Well then it's settled!" Mr. Goosen exclaims, throwing his hands in the air. "The doors are locked, but the key is in the mailbox. OH! I almost forgot. I have many trinkets and treasures throughout my house, but you must promise me you will only take *one thing*. It can be any item of special value, but once you choose to take something, that's it!"

"Just one?" Jake says. "Aww."

You all turn to look at the house. It looks like something out of a scary movie, dark and ominous.

"Good luck!" Mr. Goosen calls. "And remember, just one item!" He sounds farther away. You turn to thank him one last time... and he's gone! The three of you spin around, looking down each street, but he's nowhere in sight.

"Wow, he must have been in a hurry to move," you say.

Jake runs to the mailbox and returns with an old, iron key, red with rust.

174

You take the key and look at the house. The front porch is dilapidated, with holes in the steps and spiderwebs in the corners. The door looks like it hasn't been opened in over a year. "Which way do you want to go inside?" you ask.

"What do you mean?" Jake says. "We've got the key, let's go in the front door."

"I don't know, it looks dangerous." You point to the side of the house, where there's a small path between the wall and the woods. "We could try around back. The map says there's a back door."

Emma says, "Or the cellar. My mom and I used to help Mrs. Goosen move boxes around in the winter."

Which way will you choose when you explore...

THE HOUSE
ON
HOLLOW HILL

ABOUT THE AUTHORS

Danny McAleese started writing fantasy fiction during the golden age of Dungeons & Dragons, way back in the heady, adventure-filled days of the 1980's. His short stories, The Exit, and Momentum, made him the Grand Prize winner of Blizzard Entertainment's 2011 Global Fiction Writing contest.

He currently lives in NY, along with his wife, four children, three dogs, and a whole lot of chaos. www.dannymcaleese.com

David Kristoph lives in Virginia with his wonderful wife and two not-quite German Shepherds. He's a fantastic reader, great videogamer, good chess player, average cyclist, and mediocre runner. He's also a member of the Planetary Society, patron of StarTalk Radio, amateur astronomer and general space enthusiast. He writes mostly Science Fiction and Fantasy. www.DavidKristoph.com

Made in the USA
Middletown, DE
19 March 2017